1854 Garrett Street

1854 Garrett Street

Alfred R. Pierotti, Jr.

Writers Club Press
San Jose New York Lincoln Shanghai

1854 Garrett Street

All Rights Reserved © 2002 by Alfred R. Pierotti, Jr.

No part of this book may be reproduced or transmitted in any form or by any means, graphic, electronic, or mechanical, including photocopying, recording, taping, or by any information storage retrieval system, without the permission in writing from the publisher.

Writers Club Press
an imprint of iUniverse, Inc.

For information address:
iUniverse, Inc.
5220 S. 16th St., Suite 200
Lincoln, NE 68512
www.iuniverse.com

Any resemblance to actual people and events is purely coincidental.
This is a work of fiction.

ISBN: 0-595-22486-5

Printed in the United States of America

Acknowledgements

I would like to thank my family, extended family and friends for their support and for the encouragement they gave me during this ten-year endeavor. I would especially like to thank my wife, Cindy, my four sons, and my friend, John, who encouraged me to continue this work when I had almost given up on it. A very loving thanks to our long-ago friends and neighbors on Garrett Street, to my deceased and caring mother and father, and especially to my dear sister, Nancy.

CHAPTER 1

They were called horn toads—strange little creatures with the heads of miniature Godzilla's and the lightning-fast speed of lizards. That was my sister Nancy and my first discovery when we took up residence on 1854 Garrett Street. Much to our delight, the yard was loaded with them as well as with a few other critters—like centipedes and scorpions—that Jim Bill told us never to pick up. "They'll sting you bad," he warned us, "and it'll hurt worse than fire. They can kill you sometimes if they get you while you're sleeping. Best stay way clear of those things."

Jim Bill was two years older than Nancy and lived across the street from us. He was the first to mosey over to our new address when he picked up on all the commotion associated with our moving in.

Sandy blond hair and bright blue eyes—that was Jim Bill. He was about a foot taller than me and filled with all sorts of southwest wisdom—thunderstorms always come from thataway (the northwest), the best time to chase lightning bugs was right before sundown, and you never turned over any rocks with your bare hands. "Always use a stick," he cautioned. Jim Bill was filled with all sorts of how-tos and do's and don'ts, but they came across in a true, southern-style mode of caring. Looking back, it was Jim Bill who made Nancy's and my transition to our new home on Garrett so comfortable, exciting and easy.

What Jim Bill did for Nancy and I, his parents, Reba and Wayne Dawkins, did for my folks. Home grown Texans, the Dawkins' hospitality extended well beyond their dinner table to ours. Grits and collards, chili and rice, and fried chicken starred up at us from our paper plates the first night we moved in. During the first week, "Courtesy of the Dawkins" became as familiar a phrase around our house as their "Y'all come on over!" would later become as the days, weeks and months passed by.

But the help and friendliness extended to us by our across-the-street neighbors was soon balanced by other surprises over which my father had no control. "Oh my God!" my mother shrieked the second night after we had taken up residence. She had turned on the kitchen light and been greeted by cockroaches so big you could have saddled them up and ridden them away. This incident was followed a few nights later by a drunken Negro man trying to break down our front door—he thought his wife had locked him out of his house.

"We're getting the "biggest damn dog we can find tomorrow!" Daddy said after the police had finally left with the poor drunk. Mama was too tired to argue, but Nancy and I were delighted—the beginnings of a town-farm—like our neighbor's had—and within less than a week's time.

CHAPTER 2

If the truth be known, our move to Dallas in the early 1950's was a testament to my parent's will to get ahead—to provide something better for themselves and their children than could otherwise be had in Boston. Boston was the place where Mama and Daddy had been born and raised, where their parents had died and been buried, where my Aunt Tess was dying of cancer when we boarded the train to Texas.

Texas, they were told, was the place where Indians still conducted raids on new homesteaders, where Yankees much less Catholics were as welcome as grasshoppers, where dust storms in spring and fall choked the air from your lungs and where tornadoes would rip your house apart if the hail and thunderstorms didn't. Texas was a crazy place, no place for Bostonians. If the heat of the summer didn't get you, winter's ice and snow soon would.

Despite all of these warnings, with me in my new Hop-a-long Cassidy hat and Nancy in her Dale Evans dress, Daddy and Mama boarded the southbound train for Dallas and never looked back. It was the beginning of our journey to a new and different life in Texas.

CHAPTER 3

*E*ven at age 48, my sister, Nancy, has a number of peculiarities which are still left over from her childhood. She can write legibly with both hands at the same time, can memorize lines in a flash and can still beat all comers—young and old—in either Parcheesi or checkers—a skill she mastered on our back porch during those hot, summer afternoons when we were kids living on Garrett Street.

Nancy also has other idiosyncrasies left over from her childhood, which surface when our families get together. She scares rather easily for a grown woman, has a phobia about locking doors and hates to answer telephones. She was one of the first in line when the answering machines hit the market; and, according to her husband, she constantly offered their house as a "guinea pig" residence for any and all new alarm systems which a company might want to test.

She still has a slightly noticeable scar over her left eye, which is accentuated, only when she raises her eyebrows. On rainy or particularly cold days she'll sometimes complain about stiffness in her right knee. Her complaints will usually be followed by a mumbled, derogatory phrase aimed at the city's old sheriff or at Leon Simmons or whomever she feels at that moment was previously responsible for her present discomfort.

Two and-a half years my senior, Nancy at middle age is still attractive. Her deep, brown eyebrows accentuate her olive complexion and dark, flashing eyes. Her graying-brown hair flows in a short, gentle arch to her shoulders but never touches them. She had been a stewardess for Braniff Airlines more years ago then she cares to admit, and, for some reason, still stringently lives up to their "hair off the collar" code.

At five feet four inches tall, Nancy's figure bears only slight traces of the middle-age spread. Her stomach has a hardly noticeable roundness to it, and there is a small layer of extra skin under her chin, which by virtue of her potential wrath has defied fully doubling. Her posture is softly rigid and comfortably straight and is probably due to the training she had received during her childhood modeling days for Titche-Goettinger Department Store in Dallas.

Despite her attractive appearance and demeanor, the scar above her eye is a mark she admits runs more than skin deep. It is the one remaining outward mark, which reminds her daily of a rather ugly event in our otherwise happy and parentally sheltered childhood on Garrett Street.

"Do you still think about it?" I asked her one day.

"Just when I'm putting on my make-up," she said. "You'd think I'd be used to it by now."

My sister's passive resignation to the fact that Leon Simmons not only had existed but also had intruded upon our otherwise sedate lives at the time is still today magnified by our mother's memories of the incident. "It was hell on earth. Just awful! I look back and sometimes think we never should have moved! And to think he's still alive!"

"It was a good move," I commented. "I can't imagine a life in Boston. We'd probably have grown up in one of those tired, old two-story bungalows, perched somewhere on a crowded city side street. Subways, dirty buildings, people in your face all the time—thanks, but no thanks. I'm glad we moved. Damn glad, as a matter of fact—Leon Simmons or not!"

Such are the verbal banterings that occasionally surface when Mama Nancy and I get together. Like oil on water, the incident inevitably rises to the top only to be finally squelched by our conversation about more current events.

CHAPTER 4

*M*y father wore dark, year-round suits to the Titche-Goettinger Department Store where he worked. The old, seven-story building was located in downtown Dallas—about three miles from our house. He boarded the city bus at the end of the block early each weekday morning and was dropped off by the same bus around six o'clock that night.

The buses at that time served as one of the city's few signs of transition from its rural roots of the past to its metropolitan ideals of the future. The Interurban, as the system was called, typified our fledgling city then—always bent on moving forward despite the dusty, old roads of the past on which they were forced to run. Although downtown Dallas was but a short distance from our house, the bus ride from point to point was not as the crow flies but bore a strange resemblance to the route a confused and desperate ant might take in trying to find its way home. With clouds of black smoke belching from its tailpipes, the mechanized covered wagon snaked its way in and out and around and through the narrow neighborhood streets, pausing impatiently to pick up or let out its tired victims.

Because of its indirect route, getting back and forth to work on the bus took my father about an hour each way. Summers were the hardest for him—when the heat and dust and humidity and exhaust-fumes combined to wither his neatly pressed white shirt by mid-morning. His arrival kiss from Nancy at the bus stop that night was often met with her comment; "You're all sweaty!"

The Dallas Transit Authority was only one of the many side benefits that greeted my father when he came to Texas. Far from a teatotaler in the land of the teatotalers, he soon discovered that the nearest bottle of scotch to be purchased was eight to ten miles away and that the nearest seacoast was 425 miles due southeast. Even one of his favorite pastimes, horse racing, had been outlawed by the state of Texas some fifty years ago. During his daily bus rides to and from his office, he must have questioned on many occasions what he had gotten himself into with this move—although he never intimated any such feelings to us. When I asked him about it years later, Daddy simply stated, "You make the best decision you can, then you make it right! That's what your Mom and I did."

The Dallas of 1951 was a mixed bag of blessings and horrors. It was the year when the city's one reservoir had dropped to such disastrously low levels that drinking water had to be rationed to its citizens. It was the year which marked the closing of the swimming pool at White Rock Lake—an action made necessary due to the increased water moccasin population which, according to our city fathers, made swimming in the lake akin to committing suicide. It was the year of a raging polio epidemic that forced all children indoors when the thermometer hit ninety-five degrees or better. It was the year Aunt Tess died in Boston, when I bought my first squirt gun at Cabell's, when Daddy finally purchased a new, used car for the family and when our boxer dog, Dottie, was welcomed into our lives. Finally, it was the year of our first contact with none other than Leon Simmons.

CHAPTER 5

As best we could figure, Leon Simmons first took to Nancy from the Christmas Section that appeared in "The Dallas Times Herald's" Sunday edition. Daddy had set Nancy and I up to be models for the store's Christmas Wear and Toy promotion for the upcoming season. He brought home the paper one Sunday morning and there we were on the front page of the Fashion Section. Nancy was totally taken up with her staring role and pranced around the house like some sort of prima donna. She wouldn't talk to Jim Bill or me for days. For my part, I felt a strange sense of embarrassment since modeling according to Jim Bill was too sissy-like—unless it was for some type of new sports equipment they were trying to sell. Even that, he said, was pretty risky.

Nancy's effect on Leon must have been the slow and smoldering type. It first took the form of an almost disregarded note that was shoved underneath our front door in the middle of the night just before Christmas. Dottie charged through the window at three o'clock that morning and upset our Christmas tree. With a flurry of curses that woke Nancy and me up, Daddy threw Dottie out of the house into the car garage where she whelped and carried on frightfully. After the commotion was over, Nancy and I crawled into her bed, pulling the covers over us. We could hear Dottie crying from the car house—her yelps turning into body slams against the door of the car garage.

"I don't know who I feel sorry for the most," Nancy said, "Daddy or the dog."

As Nancy and I lay there we heard Daddy righting our Christmas tree. We heard him pick up the lamp and heard the curtains in the living room snap like a west Texas whip as they reacted to the south wind blowing in. Dottie's yelping and body slams increased as the dilapidated car garage creaked and moaned from her blows. It wasn't until we heard Daddy go outside to put some cardboard over our broken out front room window that he dropped what he was doing and went to rescue our confused Dottie. He took her out of the garage and brought her in with him.

We crawled out of bed and watched from our doorway as he petted her and talked to her. She put both her paws on his shoulders and licked him as though she'd been separated from him a thousand years. He kept talking to her even when he was putting cardboard over the window, telling her she had done good and that she was free to bust it out again if anything like this ever happened any other time. The last thing we saw Daddy do was take the piece of paper he'd gotten outside and throw it into the trash. Then he stopped for a minute, retrieved it from the wastepaper basket and put it into his pocket.

He was tired, and we knew it. He was also angry but strangely resigned in accepting the night's surprises at the same time. The dog, the prowler, the window—just a few more occurrences which had not been on his list of problems to solve at any time, much less three in the morning.

"We need to sneak that paper out tomorrow and see what it says," Nancy whispered as we crawled back into her bed. "He'll put it right in his bureau like he does all of his other papers. Dottie saw something tonight, and Daddy knows it. It must have been something important or else he wouldn't have saved it."

"Okay, okay," I muttered back. Let's go to sleep now. I'm tired." With that I shut my eyes. Nancy was still talking but I didn't pay any attention to her. I shut my eyes and shortly after my day ended.

We waited until the afternoon, when Mama was hanging the clothes on our clothesline in the backyard. Seizing the opportunity, Nancy and I sleuthed our way into our parents' bedroom and pulled the note from Daddy's top drawer.

"You keep a look out," Nancy said, "until I figure out what this says."

"Since when did you figure out how to read?"

"I know a little," she said. "If worse comes to worse I'll just copy it down and show Jim Bill. He can read it."

Nancy took what seemed forever copying the note. It's writing was jagged, and the letters were badly formed.

"Better hurry! Mama's only got a few more things to hang. She'll be coming in a minute."

"I'm going as fast as I can," Nancy said.

"Well, hurry up. She's almost through."

"I heard you the first time," she said. "I can't make anything out of some of these."

"Well, just scribble them down as close as you can."

Nancy finished just in time. The door to our backyard screen porch slammed just as Nancy was closing Daddy's bureau drawer. We scrambled into my bedroom next door. Mama came in, looked at us as for what seemed like a long minute, and then told us to go outside and play. Just then we heard Jim Bill calling us from across the street and we gladly went out front to meet him. Jim Bill had been playing football with Gary Shouts, and, even though it was just a day before Christmas, the sun was hot, and the air was humid and still. Jim Bill's hair was soaked with sweat, but when he saw Nancy coming he quickly tried to tidy himself up.

"Jim Bill," Nancy said. "Come here with us quick. We need you." To my surprise, Jim Bill immediately dropped his football in the yard and ran to her.

"What's wrong?" he asked.

"We have something to show you," she whispered, "but you can't tell anyone. We have to go someplace quiet and out of the way, some place where no one can see or hear us."

Jim Bill looked puzzled for a second as he wiped the sweat from his face with his hand. His blue eyes suddenly lit up. "Okay, we can go to our chicken coop behind the house—up in its loft. No one ever goes there this time of the day. Y'all go on back there, and I'll see you outside the coop shortly."

Nancy and I walked two houses down then cut through the neighbors' backyards until we reached the coop. The chickens squawked and carried on as though we were foxes coming after them. Feathers flew everywhere as the hens scurried to and fro knocking themselves against the chicken wire to escape.

"Some quiet place," Nancy said. "They're going to tell everyone in the neighborhood we're here."

"Hush up!" I said. "Jim Bill knows best. Besides asking him to meet with us was your idea—not his or mine."

"I guess you're right," she answered. "We might as well just sit down and wait until God knows when."

The chicken coop was located on the Dawkins' back lot, about fifty yards or so from the main house. It was separated from their immediate back yard by a straggly, post fence connected by three strands of barbed wire. Bent, rusty nails fastened the wire to a rickety, old gate that a little dirt and a lot of determination had held up for years. You never went through the gate—you always climbed over it. Jim Bill said the weight on it helped to "stabilize" it from falling down.

The chicken coop, unlike the fence, was well built. It was the length of the long screen porch on the back of our house and probably twice as wide. It had two levels. The first one was about eye-high; the second one required a short built-in ladder you had to climb to reach the loft. The floor was covered with straw, feathers and whatnot. The loft was cleaner and less smelly during the winter and mostly free of the hornet and yellow jacket nests which even Jim Bill stayed clear of during the spring and summer months.

The coop was sheltered on the north and the west by four or five bois d'arc trees which seemed to have at some point known their function but given up being excited about it some years before. Bright-green, rotting pieces of their horse apple fruit littered the ground, most by now broken into chunks, their inside pieces oozing gluey, white sap. Nancy and I had been here once before but never by ourselves. It was a strange and quiet place, a world unto itself, even though it was probably no more than a hundred yards from our front door. Nancy took the note from her pocket, tried reading it once again, then folded it up and put it back. She cleared us a place on the ground then sat down. I took my place next to her, and we waited together in silence for Jim Bill.

It seemed as though an eternity passed before Jim Bill finally arrived. We heard his jeans' legs scratch against each other as he bounded the barbed wire fence and weaved his way stealthily over to us.

"What in the world's wrong with you?" Nancy blurted out.

"Quiet!" he told her. "Mama don't know I'm here. I'm hard pressed," he explained.

"Why? What happened?" I said.

"I got in trouble," he answered. "Mama let me have it for not doing my chores."

Reba Dawkins was a good neighbor but a strict parent who had no tolerance for busted schedules. She had wailed him pretty good, and I could tell he was still feeling it. Nancy didn't know Mrs. Dawkins like I did. I had seen it one time before and didn't want any part of it. Nancy was far less sympathetic to Jim Bill's backside than me.

Nonetheless, she could tell he was coming off of a crying spell. His eyes were still a little watery and his nose, despite his trying to hide it, oozed the last bit of sinew usually associated with waning physical pain.

"Anyways," he said turning to Nancy, "what's this all about?"

"It's this." She took the note from her pocket and handed it to Jim Bill. He looked at it. "Can you read it for us, Jim Bill?" she asked.

"Yea, some of it. Where did this come from?"

"Last night some man left it on our front porch," Nancy explained. "Dottie went after him, but he got away. Daddy threw the note away then got it again from the trash can."

"Yea," I explained. "We thought it might be something important."

He studied the note. "I can't make it out very good," he said. "It's all mixed up but looky here—this looks like the word "love" but it's spelled "luv". This says "nuzpaper" but I guess it really means "newspaper". Jim Bill kept studying the paper but finally ended up shaking his head. "As for the rest of it—I just can't tell. I wouldn't worry about this anyways," he commented handing it back to her. "It's probably from some old drunk who saw you in the paper and took a liking to you."

Nancy looked more scared than ever. "But what if he comes back," she screamed out.

"Not likely he will," Jim Bill answered. "I suspect he's still running from the scare your dog put into him. At any rate, I gotta go now 'fore Mama starts looking for me again. You all had better run too. There's a blue norther headed this way, and from the looks of the sky it ain't too far away. I'll see you later!"

Jim Bill vanished as quickly as he had appeared. The sky was turning black fast and the wind started to gust fiercely. The bois d'arcs moaned under the strain and dead leaves swirled everywhere. Nancy grabbed my hand and yanked me. "Come on!" she yelled. "We'd better go home."

"Looks like Jim Bill was right about that blue norther!" I shouted above the roar of the wind.

"Seems so," Nancy yelled back. "I just hope he's right about that man too!

CHAPTER 6

❀

The big cottonwood tree that stood on our front lawn had known better than to come out. Despite the sun's rays, its stubborn leaves would have none of it. It would bend and sway with the south wind and flirt with it like a desperate lover. It would bow to the north ever so graciously then, with its back swing, beckon to the south again as if calling for its fickle lover's return. It was a wise old tree whose actions and reactions were always appropriate for the season at hand. Mama often said we could learn from it.

The Yankee rumors my parents had heard about the Texas weather were brought home to roost that Christmas Eve. Daddy had just arrived from work and had just changed clothes when we heard Mama yell "Close the windows!"

The south wind of the afternoon had quickly changed its direction to the west. Its gusts were continual and violent, and it swirled tiny particles of dust everywhere. The waning sun was barely visible and was shrouded in a cloud of yellow and amber mist. Even though all of our windows and doors were closed, the ferocious wind sent the grit through the walls. We could feel it in our throats and in our nostrils and grinding in our teeth. Daddy turned on the television just in time to hear Warren Culbertson of Channel 4 talk about what we were in store for. First the dust, he said, then the rain, then the norther, then the ice and finally the snow.

Our first Christmas Eve as well as the few days that followed saw a normal year's four seasons compressed into a matter of hours. The dust storm lasted until we sat down at our kitchen booth for dinner. The air cooler that protruded right above our heads had been turned off. The kitchen was hot and stuffy. Before we finished dinner we could hear the low rumblings of thunder in the distance. By the time Nancy and I had finished the supper dishes, the full fury of the storm had broken. It seemed to be right on top of us. Blinding flashes of lightning were followed instantaneously by deafening claps of thunder. The rain fell in sheets and assailed our windows like an angry army of liquid wasps. Dottie began yelping as though she'd been shot, finally taking refuge under Nancy's bed. A bolt of lightning hit the transformer on the telephone pole outside and white-hot sparks flew everywhere. Mama was going room to room sprinkling the house with holy water when our power finally went out.

"Better get the candles," Daddy said to me calmly. "They're in the kitchen drawer."

I handed them to Mama, and she put some in the holders on the mantle and on two other holders on the tables in the living room. When she lit them a soft, warm glow lit up the room. I've never seen her as pretty. Her skin was almost silken and her brown eyes for a moment radiated the light and warmth of the flame she had created. The five of us (Dottie included) were spending our first Christmas by ourselves—no relatives, no telephone calls, no people dropping by—in a land far away from the one we had been familiar.

The storm outside was moving on. Nancy assumed her usual place on Daddy's lap and I sat on the couch next to Mama. Dottie came up next to me and put her head on my lap. Mama wondered out loud how Aunt Alice was doing and what Uncle Jim would give her for Christmas. Daddy said something about Aunt Alba and his brother, Uncle Albert, and eventually their conversation fell off into silence.

A blustery north wind outside and an abrupt chill in the room soon replaced the serenity of the moment. Nancy and I grabbed our blankets then settled in again with our parents and Dottie. We began questioning Daddy and Mama about Santa Claus, and Mama told us a story about her favorite Christmas and about what it really meant with Jesus and everything. I understood some of it but was still worried Santa Claus was going to know we were in Dallas not Boston. Nancy told me to be quiet, and I told her maybe she didn't want her presents but I wanted mine. Then all fell silent again except for the wind. It howled under our front door like some poor spirit trying to find its way home.

Right before Nancy and I went to bed the power was restored. The lights of the tree shined above the candlelight as though it wanted us to focus upon them. Mama said it was a miracle, and Daddy seemed relieved.

"It's sleeting outside," Mama announced. "It's bed time, you two," she added. "Santa can't be very far away!"

Soon afterwards the house became pitch black. I heard the sleet and snow pelt against my window. I visited the Dawkins' chicken coop and remembered Nancy grabbing my hand as the dead leaves swirled around us. I saw the dust storm from our window again and remembered our Christmas tree lights going out. Daddy began snoring, and Nancy said something to someone in her sleep. I heard a cold, lonely dog barking far away in the night and called Dottie to me. She came and crawled up next to me. We both fell asleep together.

"Maybe your dog didn't scare him away after all."

Jim Bill and I were wading our way through the five-inch snow that had fallen overnight. I had made a bad throw with the football. It had landed underneath one of the windows to Nancy's room. He first noticed the prints and stopped dead in his tracks. He knew no one had been on this side of our house all morning.

"Look here," he said pointing to the footprints. They were large and well defined. "Seems as if whoever it was had a bad leg. See how he dragged it behind him when he walked? And look at her screen here. He went right through the wire trying to pry the latches open." He leaned over to inspect closer. "Looky here," Jim Bill said, his voice becoming excited. "He got one of them lose too."

A cold, clammy feeling came over me as I looked to where he was pointing. Two small holes just above the latches had been made in the screen.

"Nancy isn't going to like this," I said backing away. "She's scared enough as it is. Maybe it was something else that caused it."

"Like what?"

"Maybe Mama closing the windows last night."

"Nope," he answered, shaking his head. "This happened from the outside. Closing windows doesn't make footprints in the snow or cut wire screens."

Jim Bill's logic was right. The thought of someone trying to break into our house to get Nancy sent a cold shiver through me. The evidence was clear and overwhelming and terrifying. First the mysterious note and now this. "Someone's after her, Jim Bill," I whispered as though talking to myself. "Someone's trying to get her."

The happiness and joy of my first Christmas Day in Dallas had been quickly transformed into personal depression and mental paranoia. The more I thought about it, the worse the situation became. For the first time in my life I was genuinely frightened and utterly confused. Even though Nancy would be beside herself, Jim Bill had been right again. Daddy needed to know.

My worries about telling Daddy without alarming Nancy were solved Christmas evening. "Come on, son," he said getting up from his chair. "I'll take you for a ride on the sled."

He pulled me several times up and down the street then finally stopped to rest. The weather was getting to both him and me. The north wind slammed against our bodies and sent mini-swirls of snow hovering around us. It was cold. The sun had disappeared behind a bank of dark clouds, and it appeared we were in for more snow.

"Wish our house had a fireplace," he said. "Would sure feel good tonight."

"Daddy," I blurted out. "You need to see something."

"What?"

"Come over here. I'll show you."

"Lead on," he said. I led him to Nancy's window.

"Jim Bill and I noticed it this morning," I explained as we walked to the side of the house. "We thought it was pretty serious."

"There it is," I said. "Look at Nancy's window—it's been cut. Someone was trying to get her!"

He looked at the window and his eyebrows raised. "Relax," he said. "I did that the other day—forgot my key."

"Whew. I thought sure someone was after her."

"Naw," he answered. "There's no one after her, except maybe your Mama when she gets mad."

"I'm glad about that," I said. "But what about the tracks?"

"These things?"

"Yea."

"Hard to tell about them." he answered. "The morning sun's distorted them.

What else?"

"Nothing," I said both relieved and disappointed. "Just that."

Daddy and I left the sled in the driveway and walked in the waning light to our front porch. We went inside and shut the door. Behind us we left the icy, north wind, sub-zero temperatures and most of Christmas Day. Daddy had explained the cut screen and footprints away. All had, I thought, returned to normal at 1854 Garrett Street.

CHAPTER 7

It wasn't until years later that I found out that Daddy had been genuinely concerned about the screen and the footprints. He had not forgotten his key and cut the screens nor had he lightly dismissed the "distorted" footprints in the snow. He had decided to minimize the obvious that Christmas evening for fear it would alarm me. He knew I would notice if he reacted outwardly and played down the situation as best he could. He also knew I would have told Nancy—something he didn't want at all. He left the cat in the bag on purpose.

What few concerns I had about the incident melted away with the Christmas snows. Jim Bill hadn't even asked me about it. He had, however, alluded to it a few weeks afterwards—when he, Nancy and I were looking through his "Christmas" telescope at the stars one night. Nancy interrupted him and asked what he was talking about. "Your Daddy said he cut the screens trying to get in," was all Jim Bill answered. Nancy seemed confused for a moment then dismissed it in favor of a bright, shooting star that passed directly overhead.

Over the next few weeks, however, changes were made, subtle changes, which almost went by unnoticed. Daddy leisurely put deadbolts locks on the doors—a couple of weekends worth. He decided one night that we needed new screens for our windows and told Mama he had ordered them. Surprisingly enough she agreed—would help keep the bugs out," she said. He planted thorn-leafed holly bushes along the side of the house where our bedroom windows were located—despite Mr. Dawkins warning that it was way too soon—and made Nancy feed Dottie every night. He also reported the incident to the Dallas Police Department and alerted the neighbors, asking them to keep their eyes open for anything suspicious. Suddenly Mr. Dawkins understood. He offered my father his 12 gauge, but Daddy declined. He had his own 22.

Whoever or whatever it was had made my father anxious and angry at the same time. Despite what Daddy might have been feeling on the inside, his daily demeanor on the outside was normal, without even the slightest trace of concern whatsoever. Daddy was proud of himself—new locks, new screen windows, new bushes—all done secretly and with little fanfare. No one, he thought, had noticed until Nancy, perched on his lap one night, said, "Thanks, Daddy."

Whatever anxiety Nancy might have been feeling was soon buried in the excitement of her day-to-day activities. There had been no more incidents to speak of, and pretty soon Easter would be arriving. Daddy announced that we would be in "The Herald" again for Titche-Goettinger's Easter Promotion. After the pictures had been taken, she became a prima donna once again, though not so haughty this time. She talked to Jim Bill constantly about our being in the paper until I finally told her to be quiet about it and leave Jim Bill and me to ourselves.

"Don't be so hard on her," Jim Bill said to me in front of her one afternoon. "Being in the paper's a mighty special thing."

"That isn't what you told me before," I commented. "You said it was stupid. Remember?" They both ignored my comment and pretty soon Nancy and Jim Bill were wrapped-up in their own private conversation as they walked around the back yard together. Nancy took his hand once and talked and smiled and giggled until I finally felt ignored enough to leave them to themselves.

I went to our front yard and discovered our wise, old cottonwood had been tricked. The warm, mid-March sun had coaxed the tree's blossoms into coming out early. I lay down on the brown grass and looked up at the wispy clouds sliding northwards against the powdery blue sky. At some point during my stay there I came to realize that Jim Bill, at least for that afternoon, liked Nancy more than me. A force more powerful than our friendship had been at work, and something inside told me there was not one thing I could do about it.

The phone rang and shortly afterward Mama called me in to get ready. "That was Daddy," she announced. "We're going to the Savoy's tonight for dinner. You and your sister's Easter pictures are in. Daddy said the Savoys want to see them, too. He said they came out wonderful."

"Do we have to tonight?"

"Yes!" Mama answered. "Go call your sister and tell her to come in. You both need to get ready. Daddy will be here soon."

In the early fifties, White Rock Lake had been Dallas' only reservoir. It was not a natural lake or a big lake but was at the time the city's only claim to a "significant body of sustained water" larger than an oversized pond. It was the city's only oasis and was created in the mid 1940's to ease water shortage problems which had existed and would come up undoubtedly in the future. White Rock was created in the knick of time, as it became the city's only source of water during the draught, which began in 1951 and ended some four years later. White Rock, however, was viewed by many Dallasites as a strange lake.

Located in East Dallas, at times it seemed as though it regretted its own existence—as though it felt out of place in its alien locale. Its waters breathed with the seasons. They would swell with the spring rains then collapse under the hot, summer sun, exposing the tops of its underwater stumps like the gigantic ribs of a starved corpse. Lawther Drive, a narrow, two-lane road that belted the lake, ribboned its shoreline. The surrounding land gave way to rolling, higher ground on the lake's eastern side where expensive estates had been built to overlook the water. The lake's west side was a tangled mass of ancient trees and thick underbrush. This night would be our first formal introduction to White Rock Lake and to the Savoys.

The Savoy's house was nestled among large trees and stood about seventy-five yards back from Lawther Drive. The house was a neatly painted two-story affair, sprawling north to south on its large lot. The back of the house faced the street and its driveway twisted around the trees and finally ended up on the opposite side of the house in front of its main entrance. From this point the lake looked as though you could reach out and touch its waters.

We had often heard our father talk about Mr. Savoy around our house. He was Dad's counterpart at Neiman Marcus and it wasn't long before the common trials and tribulations of their jobs as display directors made them the best of friends. They were both personal friends and professional rivals since Dallas' three major department stores—Tithe Goettinger, Sanger Harris and Neiman Marcus—were constantly competing for a bigger share of their consumers' pocketbooks.

Guy Savoy was a friendly and jovial man but also a smart one. He was a man of mystery and intrigue to both Nancy and me. He had a round, moon-shaped face and a thin hairline, which had already begun receding on top. He was short of stature and stocky in build and bore a thick, black moustache that seemed like it needed to be cut on the bottom when he smiled. His hazel eyes sparkled when he spoke and lit-up with each thought. They looked not only at you but also, it seemed, through you as though he were anticipating your reaction before it actually happened.

Although married for some twenty-three years, the Savoys lived by themselves as they had no children. Nevertheless, they took an instant liking to Nancy and me and went out of their way to make us feel wanted and welcomed.

Dinner that evening was a "remarkable" event, according to Nancy years later. There was no familiar drone of the overhead water cooler, nor the drab flower-paste wallpaper of our kitchen on Garrett. Instead of a booth, we sat around an elegant dining room table meticulously ordained with crystal glasses filled with water and wine. Each plate was balanced on either side with lots of forks and several knives and spoons that told me I'd better be on my best behavior.

Nancy and I sat and ate and stared through the dining room's large rectangular picture window which, in turn, stared incessantly and uninterruptedly out upon White Rock Lake. It was dusk.

"God that was good, Thelma!" Mr. Savoy commented pushing his plate away from him. "I'm stuffed!" He paused for a moment then looked pensively out the window. "This is the type of night when she usually comes out," Mr. Savoy commented as though he were thinking out loud. "See those leaves blowing in the wind?" he asked looking at Nancy and me. "Could mean she's close." Silence filled the room.

"Not tonight, Guy. Maybe some other time." Daddy finally said.

"No, no, Hal," he shot back. "She's just as real as those dark clouds coming towards us over the lake. We've seen her—Thelma and I have, and we swear by what we've seen." His eyes were trained on Daddy and almost popping out of their sockets.

"Guy," Thelma said. "Let's drop it. Now's not a good time."

"No!" Nancy suddenly blurted out. "Tell us now. We're not afraid!"

"Guy!" Thelma warned.

"It's okay—isn't it Daddy?"

Daddy tossed his napkin gently on the table in exasperation. "I guess," he said. "But make it light, Guy. I want the kids to get some sleep tonight."

Guy nodded.

"What are you talking about anyway?" Nancy blurred out.

"Nancy!" Mama said. "Mind your manners!"

"It's okay," Mr. Savoy said. "You look a little like her, you know—long brown hair, deep brown eyes—the daughter I never had. I watch for her on nights like this—to see if she'll come again. She never has yet. We call her the Lady of the Lake because we first encountered her by the lake. She was upset and worried and desperate for a ride. She was young—maybe sixteen—and was wearing a white, formal gown that was soaked to her skin by the night's rain. By the time we happened on her it was well after midnight. The rain was teeming down so hard we scarcely noticed her. We stopped. She got in. She thanked us for picking her up and asked us to drop her off at an address on Gaston Avenue. She offered no explanations only appreciation. At first her breathing was forced, but, it seemed the nearer we came to her address, there was no sound of her breathing at all."

'This it?' I asked the lady.

No reply.

'Is this where I turn?' I asked again.

Thelma looked towards the back and let out a start. The girl had vanished. Confused and tired, I wanted to go home and call it a night. Thelma, however, insisted we stop.

We turned into the driveway and wound our way through the pitch-black darkness towards the house. It laid about 100 yards back from the deserted avenue and, as we pulled to a stop the rain began teeming down again.

'Go on,' Thelma coaxed. 'I'll wait here.'

I walked as fast as I could to the front porch and rang the bell. The driving rain was stinging me, and I was soon drenched to the skin. I waited for signs of life from within but there were none. I rang the bell again—twice this time and waited.

A bolt of lightning lit up the sky as the door flew open. Startled, I jumped back then tried to compose myself as best I could. A silhouette of medium stature stood before me.

'What do you want!' he growled. 'Are you mad?'

'I've come about your daughter,' I said.

'What's that you're saying?'

"I've come about your daughter,' I yelled, trying to be heard above the storm. 'We gave her a ride here tonight. She was caught out in the storm. She said this is where she lives. We don't know where she went.'

'I have no daughter!' he yelled. Another lightning bolt struck as he said this. His fist was raised. His eyes were raging, his face gaunt and drawn. His long, white hair frayed in every direction.

'My wife and I picked her up at the lake no more than ten minutes ago. She gave us this address. When we got here she had vanished.'

'I have no daughter,' he blurted out again. 'Not any more.'

'This is 1654 Gaston, isn't it?'

'Get out of here and leave me alone!' he yelled. 'I know your type. You like to see people squirm in their misery—you thrive on it don't you! Calling on me this time of night—especially tonight. What kind of a man are you? Get out of here and leave me alone or I'll call the police! By God I'll call them!' I was flabbergasted.

'But the girl.' I protested. 'What about her?'

'There is no girl!' he yelled back at me. 'You. You and all the rest. I'll tell you what I told them. She died, Sir! Two years to this date. There is no girl I tell you—not any more.'

'I'm sorry,' I said. 'But then who was she—the girl in my car? How did she know to come to this address?'

'She is dead!' he scowled. 'She drowned in the lake. She is no more—can't you people understand that? Get out of here!' he yelled again. 'Get out of here and leave me alone! Just let me be.'

He shut the door as though it weighed a thousand pounds and left me standing dumbfounded on his porch. A chill passed through me as I walked half-stunned back to my car.

Thelma and I went home, but we never forgot the incident nor did we ever return to the house on Gaston Avenue. The girl left a watermark on the seat of my car—where she was sitting. It's still here to this day."

"On special nights, when the wind howls and the rain comes down in sheets and the lightning flares an angry sky, she returns to the lake looking for God knows who or what. We've never seen her again, though others claim they have. Just the same, though, Thelma and I keep watching. She is a beautiful but tormented soul seeking some type of relief, which this world will never give her."

Nancy and my first visit was our last visit to the Savoy's house. Nancy insisted on seeing the watermark on the upholstery of Mr. Savoy's car before we left. Having seen it, she stayed quiet for the remainder of the night. Something had finally rendered her speechless.

The storm, which broke over White Rock that evening, was followed by another and another. The rain and wind and lightning lasted well past the time I fell asleep. The violence outside wasn't what woke me up that night. Rather, it was the movement of the bed as someone crawled in and hugged me. "Mama?" I asked half asleep. "No," came the answer. "It's just me."

Of all my recollections about Garrett Street this is perhaps my warmest. It was the first time my sister, Nancy, came to me for a quiet type of help and support. She cried softly for a little while, then turned over. I stayed awake until I was sure she was asleep, then closed my eyes to join her.

CHAPTER 8

The persistent thunderstorms of our first spring in Dallas came and went, and, like the Easter candy we were given, soon disappeared. So did our immediate terror of the Lady. She was there—then she wasn't there—always appearing as some misty, shadowy figure in the backs of our minds.

Summer came early that year, and the high humidity coupled with the presummer heat made our house feel like a steam bath. The air cooler droned endlessly but, it seemed, to no avail. One scarcely noticed when summer officially came that year as May and June seemed like one prolonged heat spell.

Nancy, Jim Bill and I whiled away the hours of these hot, lazy days either playing Checkers or Parcheesi on our back porch, or, when that ran out, playing silly acting games in the backyard at Nancy's insistence. Nancy decided she was going to be an actress, a decision she made right after she saw herself again in the Easter Section of "The Herald". She even went so far as to even have Mama help her memorize some of Juliet's lines from "Romeo and Juliet"; and she pranced around the back yard saying them over and over again as though she was some kind of Texas Shirley Temple. She insisted that Jim Bill learn lines as well. At first he balked, but finally she wore him down so much he ended up giving in.

Jim Bill was Nancy's special friend—her boy-lover. He'd show up every summer morning and wouldn't leave until his Mama called him—usually after lunch. The three of us enjoyed hanging out with each other—especially Nancy and Jim Bill. As much time as they spent together, they never fought or argued. Jim Bill was ever the gentleman and accepted her occasional bossiness as signs of her affection for him. Nancy often remarked that I needed to act more like Jim Bill.

The summer, which started so early that year, continued mercilessly. The grass browned, the flowers wilted on their stems and by July even the trees were bowing under the summer surge. Because of the lack of rain, the city limited the use of water to people only, rather than yards and shrubs, a step which city fathers warned might later be followed by the discontinuance of such "conveniences" as water coolers and the like. Public swimming pools were shut down and soon afterwards the city began rationing water to its citizens.

Rain (or the lack of it) was not the only worry that was on people's minds. An invisible and deadly killer reared its ugly head that year and relentlessly preyed on victims all over Dallas. The polio epidemic, thought to be intensified by the prolonged and excessive heat, raged throughout the city. Medical authorities urged residents to keep their children inside, especially when temperatures reached or exceeded 95 degrees. Normally rational citizens were panic stricken, so much so that active neighborhoods like ours looked like ghost towns from early afternoon until after dusk. I remarked about how deserted it seemed once. Mama retorted "Everyone stays inside now—everyone with any sense."

Shortly afterwards Nancy and I were rolling marbles on the top of Mama's washing machine when we heard a vaguely familiar voice call out from down the street. It was Mr. Ortiz, the ragman! Mama shook her head for a reason I didn't understand as Nancy ran to the sugar jar, pulled out a stuck-together lump, then flew out the door. "So much for having sense," Mama muttered to herself.

At first Nancy and I had been afraid of Ortiz. We had never seen anyone like him before. His skin was weather-beaten like old, dried-out leather. A scraggly, grey beard that cascaded down his cheeks to below his chin accentuated the lines in his face. His shirt was never ironed and his trousers always seemed too big. He wore a dark brown sombrero that shadowed his head like a huge umbrella. Despite all that, he was Dallas' last door-to-door rag merchant, he always told us in broken English. When he died the "rag" profession, as he knew it, would be no more.

Ortiz's head always drooped low upon his chest as though the sun's bright glare was too much for his tired eyes. His body jerked sporadically, the loose springs of his bare, wooden seat long since worn out by the bumps and jolts of the same path he had traveled for years. For all practical purposes, he could have dropped the reins and let his little mule steer the course. It knew today's route just as well as he did.

Jasper, his mule, had had a long day. The dogs had been cruel to him. They had torn at his heels viciously and made them bleed. His old master had haphazardly shooed the dogs away, but there was always another and another. Finally his master had grown tired and like always, given up.

Ortiz and Jasper had their schedules. They would show up every summer then disappear with the first cold spell. They would come down Garrett Street when the summers' heat made them thirsty—when they needed our water—then meander to and fro down endless side streets until they felt like going home. Their route was always the same yet never the same. A consistent type of inconsistency was their norm. Their sight was always a surprise yet never a surprise—just enough to break up the day's monotony when they showed up.

They came to our street by way of Ross Avenue, ignoring the heat and the dust and the car-fumes and the squawking horns. They would hold their worn course—half on the pavement, half on the brown, sun-baked grass—as though their creaking wagon was hitched to some invisible track below. They would turn on Garrett Street and then stop for a short while. He'd call out "Rags" in a harsh, raspy voice then wait.

"The rag man Mama!" I yelled. "Hurry up! "Nancy's already gone!"

"I know, I know," she answered handing me some old clothes. "Give him these."

I darted out the door after Nancy and saw she and Dottie had already arrived at Jasper and Ortiz. I gave Mr. Ortiz my rags, and he nodded thanks.

"Jasper's looking awfully tired," Nancy said as she stroked the mule. "Look—his hoofs are bleeding."

Ortiz bent over and looked then shrugged his shoulders. "The dogs," he said. "Too many to fight. Old mule—he's tired like me." Ortiz bent over and looked again. "He will heal."

"Poor Jasper," Nancy said. "He's so skinny. Mr. Ortiz! You can see his ribs!"

"I no eat, he no eat. These days grow hotter now. We both not hungry anyway. Here," Ortiz said, reaching his hand out to Nancy. "For you and your hermanito. How do you say—rock candy? No chew, though—too hard. Put in mouth—no chew. Come up," he said motioning to Nancy. "You drive."

Nancy climbed aboard the rickety wagon and flicked the reins. Jasper nudged forward slowly and, like he'd always done before, stopped when he reached the front of our house.

This day Mama came out with water, and, as she approached, Mr. Ortiz tipped his sombrero to her. He grumbled something in Mexican then took the glass and drank what seemed like forever.

"Get the hose," Mama said turning to me, "and wash off Jasper's feet. He needs some water too." Mama looked and shook her head at Ortiz. "Don't know how you two do it," she commented. "All day everyday in this terrible heat."

"I am the last rag man in Dallas," Ortiz responded, without looking at her. "When I leave the rag business is over." Mama nodded then turned to go in.

"Mr. Ortiz," she called. "I'll have some more rags for you next week." Ortiz tipped his hat again and bid us good-bye. We stroked Jaspar once more then stood back as the wagon eked forward. The Shouts' dogs darted out from between two houses and began nipping Jasper's hooves. The mule reared and tried to kick them off but was unsuccessful.

"Get 'em, Dottie!" Nancy yelled. True to form, Dottie did as she was told. The blonde bolt of lightning snarled her way past the wagon to Jasper. The mule's attackers soon vanished across the street with their tales between their legs. Jaspar stopped, bent his head down to Dottie, then lifted it again and pulled. He and his ally had at last scored a victory today.

Nancy and I watched from the curb as the wagon became smaller and smaller. Then it stopped and turned around and began coming back towards us. When he was close enough, Ortiz waived for us to come. He was holding a long, white envelope in his hand.

"For you," he said thrusting it towards Nancy. "Forgot to give." Nancy took the envelope and looked at it. She was dumbfounded. She recognized the writing. "Good news, maybe," Ortiz commented as he turned Jaspar around again. "Good news, maybe."

We could tell by our shadows it was noon and before long we could hear Mama calling to us to come in for lunch. We shrugged her call off and stood as motionless as the trees around us. Ortiz' wagon once again became smaller. Little did Nancy and I realize that we were witnessing the last fading images of the door-to-door rag business in Dallas.

CHAPTER 9

"Antlions are strange, little critters" commented Jim Bill. He, Nancy and I were sitting in a circle watching one burrow its way through our back yards' topsoil. "Watch him. He'll dig a bit then spit it out—see there? He's throwing dirt out." Minute particles of dirt flew a fraction of an inch above the surface as his hole became bigger and bigger. "When he's through digging he'll hide himself under the dirt and wait for an ant to come along. Then he'll pounce on it and drag it underneath and eat it." Nancy squirmed a bit then got up. Jim Bill's comment had hit a little too close to home.

Nancy hadn't opened the note given to her by Ortiz the day before nor did she know what to do with it. She acted as though she had never received it—like the whole incident was a type of dream she wanted to forget. I was surprised. She hadn't talked to me about it or even asked Jim Bill to read it like she had with the first note we had snuck from Daddy's drawer. Even though she never mentioned it, her reaction to Jim Bill's comment told me she felt something strange was going on, something that was unfamiliar and way beyond her control. She walked around the backyard then turned and went inside.

Nancy kept to herself for days, but they seemed like years. Jim Bill would rehearse his lines in front of her in the backyard, yet she would have none of it. She'd scowl and dismiss him as though he had never existed. She wouldn't eat or drink. She'd go through the motions of the hot summer days as though she were separated from them. When Dottie, her favorite, came to her, she'd treat her as though she was just something else that complicated her life. Mama and Daddy hadn't noticed. They were worried about Aunt Tess in Boston.

The heat, the endless, summer heat droned on. Daddy brought home some fans to cool us off but they only blew around the hot air already in the house. Nerves frayed, tempers peaked, then Mama learned Tess was on death's doorstep. She broke down, bought a ticket to Boston with what little savings we had left, kissed us a regretful good-bye and left.

Daddy had made previous arrangements with LD to watch us during the day. She was a lady who came to him highly recommended by the Dawkins.' She was to give us breakfast and lunch, make sure we came in when it got too hot and keep an eye on us. She was a heavy-set black lady who moved our floors when she walked. She always talked as though she was carrying on a conversation with herself, but we soon learned half the time she was talking to us. She was good-natured and caring and a stickler for neatness. She also showed us the southern way to keep cool by placing a rolled-up wet towel on the backs of our necks.

It was strange having LD at first. We had never seen a black person up close before. The hair on her arms was curly and frayed, and she talked with a different accent than Ortiz. The palms of her hands were white, and her eyes seemed at times a little watery and bloodshot. I was going to ask her about it once but Nancy quickly shut me up. "Use your manners for a change," she said.

Dottie was LD's favorite. She'd feed her scraps from breakfast and lunch and would talk to Dottie as though she was the last dog alive on earth. Dottie would wag her tail at LD and follow her around. She'd talk to Dottie like Daddy—as though she was human—and we liked her for that. When the day was done, she'd call Dottie to her and Dottie would come.

Foremost among all of LD's qualities was her ability to bake pies. Their aroma filtered all over the neighborhood and soon brought orders from both the Dawkins, the Shouts and from almost all our other neighbors. Her customers would show up on our front porch at all hours of the day, pay Nancy for their goodies, then go home. When we helped LD she would pay us a nickel each. When we didn't, LD would talk to us even more. LD served as a welcomed distraction to Nancy and the note. She had made Nancy forget it for a time, find herself, then proceed. Before long we learned Tess had finaly died and that Daddy would be going to Boston to join Mama for the funeral. LD had agreed to stay.

The Dawkins drove Daddy and us to Love Field to see him off. Daddy was as upset as we were. Tears filled his eyes as he gave us a hug good-bye. This was not something he had wanted to do. "Mind LD," he said. "I'll call to see how you are doing."

Mr. Dawkins took us to the lookout deck to see Daddy's plane leave. One propeller started, then coughed, then started again. The next did the same, and finally the last two joined in. It was pushed slowly out of its parking spot, and then all four engines roared as the plane inched forward. It slowly made its way to the end of the runway then thunder and a cloud of white smoke broke lose. Before long the plane was airborne, leaving us far behind.

"LD will take good care of you," Mr. Dawkins said as he walked us back to his car. "If she doesn't, we're just across the street."

The absence of our parents drew Nancy and I even closer together. Although we understood Tess was dying, the event placed us secondary to it. We felt strangely neglected and alone. They had gone and left us behind. Even Dottie paced back and forth sniffing and whining for long stretches at a time. At first Nancy and I had decided to take up residence in her room until Mama and Daddy returned, and we'd comfort our poor Dottie by having her sleep with us at night.

LD tried to discourage this at first. Then, after our prodding, she finally agreed.

Two days after Mama and Daddy left the Dawkins invited Nancy and I to dinner. Jim Bill announced it that morning in our backyard and said that his Mama was making something special, and we'd better eat it. "I probably won't be hungry," Nancy said. "Not at all."

"Better eat it anyway," Jim Bill answered back. "Make like you're really liking it—even though you're not. Mama's real proud about her cooking. She likes food that has vitamins and bulk—the kind that has your natural processes built into it. I know you'll both like it," Jim Bill said pleadingly. "I eat it all the time."

Nancy shrugged her shoulders when I told Jim Bill we'd come. His eyes sparkled, as he looked at Nancy, then dimmed at what he saw. She turned and went inside and started crying to LD. LD stopped what she was doing, took Nancy in her arms and let her sob. She rocked Nancy back and forth ever so gently and consoled her. Nancy left for a moment, came back with the note and handed it to LD. LD opened it, read it and came to the back door. "Jim Bill!" she yelled. "You all come in now." When we got in I heard her tell Jim Bill "We're eating here tonight. Go tell your Mama that. Tell her to send your Papa over here too—just as soon as he gets home!"

Mr. Dawkins knocked on our door right after sundown that evening. He was in a terrible state. His voice was raspy and almost nonexistent. His eyes bulged, his breath wheezed, his body sagged as though it were under a thousand pounds of pressure. He carried with him a dish that he said his wife was bent on him delivering to us. He handed it to LD, talked to her for a moment, then told LD to call him if there was any trouble. LD had pulled the note out of her pocket to show him, but he was in such a reduced state that it would not have made any difference anyway. She stuffed it back into her pocket and told him goodnight. We watched out the front window as Mr. Dawkins slowly trekked his way over our front yard, across the street and finally to his front door. The door closed, the front porch light went out and instantaneously everything outside turned dark.

"Praise Jesus!" LD yelled, raising her arms to heaven. "You're life is in my hands!" Nancy and I ran to LD to see what all the commotion was. She had just uncovered Mrs. Dawkins dish—brussels sprouts, collards, liver and onions. The fumes from it ran through the house like a poisonous gas. Even Dottie, who had missed her feeding time by two hours, shrank from it in favor of the heat outside.

We all soon joined Dottie on the back porch. The locusts were still loud and boisterous. Lightning bugs flitted around the yard, first here, then there. A breeze from the south came up and stayed with us a while, like our thoughts about Mama and Daddy, Ortiz and Jaspar, Tess and the airplane that took Mama and Daddy away from us. LD finally sat down in our old rocking chair and took us to her lap. "That note," she said looking at Nancy," Well I don't quite know what to make of it.

"Is it scary?" Nancy asked.

"Not really. It's just peculiar. Do you want to see it?"

Nancy shook her head no.

"I do," I said.

"You and your Daddy can read it together—if he lets you," LD replied. "Until then let's us just put it in the backs of our minds and enjoy the evening."

CHAPTER 10

Dottie slobbered when she slept outside. The parched ants, being so thirsty, would follow the saliva trail to her mouth in search of the moisture flow. When they found it, Dottie would lick her lips, swallow them up, and then go back to sleep.

Dottie was the key to worry-free living, LD often remarked as she slaved over our stove. "Do what you can, then leave the rest for tomorrow," she always told us. LD, however, never practiced what she preached. She baked morning, noon and night trying to fill the orders for her pies. We helped her as much as we could but soon pooped out. She finally threw down her apron one night and said that was enough. The heat had finally gotten to her too.

It was mid-July and still no rain. Mama and Daddy, we learned, would be home as soon as they could after Aunt Tess' funeral. Jim Bill was once again a frequent visitor in the mornings, and Nancy and I and he resumed our day-to-day living as though the note had never existed. LD had been successful in warding off the Dawkins' dinner invitations and, in her usual worldly wisdom, had begun serving cold cuts and fruit for our meals rather than hot, oppressing suppers that laid on our stomachs for hours. LD would not let us out of her sight. Like an over-protective hen, she showed up every place we were, then vanished, then showed up once more. Jim Bill said she was "truly pretty remarkable". Even he couldn't tell where she would be next.

Nighttime, after dinner, would usually find us on our back porch listening to the lonely locusts winding down their songs as the crickets and frogs started theirs up. To us it was a little scary once Jim Bill went home. Our whole backyard seemed to be alive with foreboding sounds that weren't there during the day. We'd look out into the black and wait for LD.

At last she'd come, her soiled white dress and apron a testament to her day of labor around the house. Our rocking chair would moan as she squeezed her way into it.

Finally, when she was set, she'd call us to her. Her lap was warm and soft, but strangely never hot. She'd hug Nancy and I and hum sad songs that never had words. The sounds of the night were her background and she, it seemed, was the star.

"Your Mama and Papa will be coming back the day after tomorra," she announced to us one night after she'd finished her singing.

"Will you stay?" I asked pleadingly.

She shook her head no. "Lord knows I wished I could. I'm goin' to miss you two." She sighed. "Look here," she said, "Your sister's already asleep—a little princess if I ever saw one," she said shaking her head.

"Will we ever see you again, LD?"

"I hope so," she sighed. "I really do."

"What will you do? Where will you stay?"

"Here." she said. "Help me with your sister." LD struggled up from the rocking chair. "Don't you worry. I'll be all right. Good folks like the Dawkins' are mighty kind to me. Maybe I'll drop in sometime and visit you two every once in awhile," she added. "We'll worry 'bout that tomorra. Right now it's time to go to bed."

LD tucked Nancy, Dottie and me in Nancy's bed. I heard her walk to the kitchen, turn on the water cooler and utter a small moan. She murmured, it seemed, to someone for a long time. I thought it was Dottie until I realized Dottie was still lying with us. The kitchen light burned brightly for a while, then the cooler was turned off, and LD walked to her bed. She sniffed twice then looked in on us again. She bent over and kissed Nancy's cheek then mine. She stared at us for a long second then turned and left the room. We would miss LD.

Someone poked me in the ribs. I rolled over and opened my eyes. It was still night but the moon was full, spreading a dim light both inside and out. I felt the poke again and realized it was Nancy.

"What do you want?"

"Be quiet," Nancy barely whispered. "There's someone out there—outside my window."

I looked at the two windows opposite us. They both were open with their shades drawn halfway down. "I don't see anything," I whispered back. "You must be dreaming."

I looked at Dottie. She was sprawled out sound asleep across the bottom of the bed and was snoring a little.

"That window over there," Nancy said pointing. "I saw a shadow. It's gone now."

The night was lonesome but far from silent. The Shouts and their church choir were just finishing practice for their church's service this Sunday. The singing finally stopped, and the members prayed a long prayer and left. Some of them laughed as they came out of the house. Several of them commented on how stifling the night air was. Car engines started, and the reflections of the car lights made shadows dance across the walls of Nancy's room. The lights gradually dimmed as the car-noise finally faded. The night once again fell silent and calm.

"There's nothing out there," I half-whispered starring at the window she had pointed to. "Probably from the Shouts' next door."

"It was not," Nancy insisted. "It looked like the shadow of a man's chest and head—he had a hat on. It stood there—looking in, not moving at all."

I leaned up on my elbow and stared at the window. "You sure you just weren't seeing things? I don't see any shadow."

"Yes I'm sure," she answered. "I told you it's not there now. It's gone."

"Okay, okay—it's gone now. Dottie didn't hear anything—look at her. She's still asleep. She'd know if someone were out there. You just had a bad dream—go back to sleep." Nancy rolled over on her side to avoid seeing the window.

I propped myself on one elbow again and peered at the window through the dimly lit room. The white, cloth shade hung motionlessly in the stagnant night air. A mosquito buzzed by my ear then around my head then flew off. I lay back down and listened to the monotone chirping of the crickets outside the window. I heard Nancy's breathing become heavier. She had managed to fall right back to sleep. In the meantime she had left me lying open-eyed and wide-awake. The more I tried to bring on sleep the more frustrated and angry I became, and I began plotting in detail what I would do to her tomorrow to get even. I was midway through my plan when something jarred me back to reality. The crickets had gone silent. I opened my eyes and looked at the window. The shadow was standing directly in front of it. It stood motionless for a few seconds, as if it were listening for something, then crouched down on one knee. My heart was pounding in my ears. I heard the sound of the screen's wire being cut. So did Dottie.

Dottie bounded from the bed and flew at the window. She was barking and snarling like I've never heard her before. I pulled Nancy from bed, and we both ran to LD. LD was already up and heading down the hall towards us. Somehow through the hallway's darkness she latched on to us and drew us close to her. "Both of you wait right here!" she said. "Don't move!"

By now Dottie was in a frenzy. "Come on," Nancy cried to me. "It's not going to hurt my dog!"

We ran back to Nancy's room and tripped over something on the floor. It was LD. She was yelling at the top of her lungs "Git outta here, Mista! Git outta here!" Dottie had leapt half way through the screen and had a hold of the shadow's arm. Her back legs were writhing in mid air as she tried to get leverage on the window's small ledge. The shadow kept hitting her again and again but she wouldn't let loose. Glass shattered as the window shade flew across the room. The nightstand crashed into the wall as the lamp on it splintered and sent glass flying everywhere. Finally we heard Dottie yelp in awful pain. She let go and the shadow, now a retreating silhouette in the moonlight, slipped across the Shouts' back yard and disappeared into the night.

"Turn on a light! Turn on a light!" yelled LD. I ran to the hallway switch just outside Nancy's room and flipped it.

"Dottie!" Nancy shrieked, running over to her. The dog was lying on splinters of broken glass and bleeding. Her head was raised. Her mouth was oozing blood and white foamy saliva. LD had managed to get to her feet. She was aghast at the sight before her.

"Nancy, honey, let the dog be, now. Your bleeding, honey—your feet. Let the dog be now. Just stay right there. I'm coming over to get you." LD walked to her and picked her up.

Both bottoms of Nancy's feet were dripping blood. "Come sit on the bathtub while I draw you some hot water. I'm going to put some baking soda in it so's it might hurt a little. You keep your feet in the water anyway 'til I get back. Don't you worry about your doggie," she said. "I'll take care of her—she'll be alright. Little 'un," she said turning to me, "you stay here with your sister. There are some things I gotta do."

LD's "gotta do" list that night lasted well into the early morning hours. She immediately called Dr. Berger, then the police and Mr.

and Mrs. Dawkins. Shouldering his 12-gauge shotgun, Mr. Dawkins was the first to arrive.

LD refused to let Dr. Berger treat her until he had not only tended to Nancy but also to Dottie. We didn't know until later that LD had bruised her shoulder and hip from her fall and had slivers of glass lodged in her feet and hands from the broken lamp fragments. Dottie had cuts all in her mouth from being hit so many times and a puncture wound in her right front shoulder where she had been stabbed by something short and pointed—like a pocketknife. The police arrived and asked Nancy and I all sorts of questions—did we see whom it was, how big was the man, what'd he look like and so on. Neither of us could answer them very plainly.

LD produced the note that was given to Nancy by Ortiz, and told the short, stout policeman in charge the story behind it. He looked at it briefly then put it down on one of the tables in the living room. "Robbery," I heard him tell Mr. Dawkins, "robbery was why he was here. Nobody home but the niggress and the kids. Easy pickings' is what he thought. He won't be back. That mutt there got a good piece of him I'll bet."

"She's not a mutt!" Nancy yelled at him. "She's Dottie!"

"That's right, Sheriff," Dr. Berger said. "That mutt, as you call her, probably saved these children's lives."

The Sheriff looked at Dr. Berger, then at Nancy. "Excuse me, little lady," he said, tipping his Stetson. "I stand corrected." Nancy turned her face away.

The night's surprise party at 1854 Garrett Street. finally ended. Assuring us we'd all survive, Dr. Berger soon left, then the Sheriff and his posse, and finally Mrs. Dawkins. Mr. Dawkins, whose cold must have by now gone into pneumonia, was determined to hang around awhile until things "settled down" a bit. When I awoke the next morning he was the first one who greeted me from our living room chair. He had stayed all night.

CHAPTER 11

The news of the break-in amplified for Mama and Daddy an already bad situation. First Tess's death, which Mama had taken especially hard, then this bad news. They had been notified by the Dawkins' of what had transpired and had caught the first plane home.

Not wanting to alarm them any more than necessary, Mrs. Dawkins had kept the details to a minimum. She had simply told them the bare facts—that someone tried to break into the house, that Nancy's feet had been cut a bit by some broken glass and that Dottie had chased off the burglar. She said LD had fallen and hurt her shoulder but was up and around and functioning "real fine".

When Mama and Daddy finally arrived and walked through our front door, their faces dropped in disbelief. Before them stood Nancy, whose ankles and feet, with the exception of her toes, were completely bandaged; LD, whose arm was in a sling; and Dottie, whose wrapped upper body was so stiff she had to hobble up to them on three legs to give them her official hello. Daddy's first words were "Jesus Christ".

Mama's reaction was a little calmer, though her eyes were all teary. She took us in her arms and almost squeezed the life out of us. She hugged LD and petted Dottie then sat down on the edge of the couch and tried to compose herself as best she could. "What happened?"

she asked looking at us. "You look like you've been through…" she shrugged her shoulders…"hell".

"Not quite hell, ma'am," LD said, "but mighty close to it. You ought to be mighty proud of them, ma'am, and that dog there, too. We all had quite a night last evening."

"Well," Mama said looking at Daddy. "Let your father and I get changed. Then we can all sit down, and you can tell us all about it."

It was late afternoon. The brassy, Texas sun was setting behind some disappointed thunderheads and sending purple, pink and red streaks across an approaching indigo sky. It wasn't long before we were all sitting together in front of our portable fans in the living room, hashing out the events of the previous night.

My mother never ceased to astound me. She listened attentively as our story unfolded, and, unlike Daddy, reserved her comments. She nodded as we gave an account of the shadow at the window, the screen being cut and finally the fight between Dottie and the shadow. Nancy broke in more often than not with her dramatics and finally ended it all by looking at me and saying, "I told you I saw a shadow." LD got the note and handed it to Daddy. He looked at it and commented how the writing was so bad he could hardly read it. Then he handed it to Mama for her to look at.

"Mr. Ortiz delivered it to Nancy the last time he came by," I said. "He almost forgot. Didn't he, Nancy?" Nancy nodded. "He had to turn his wagon all the way around from the end of the block. I think he thought it was something good—like a surprise."

"Some surprise," Daddy commented under his breath. "We'll get this all taken care of," he assured us. "No need to be overly worried."

"That fat old policemen called Dottie a mutt," Nancy suddenly blurted out of nowhere. "I hate that man," she said stroking Dottie's head. "You should have bit him too, girl."

The conversation late that Wednesday afternoon purposefully drifted away from its original starting point and on to a variety of other subjects. It wandered back and forth from my parents' trip to

Boston and Tess's death, back to Dallas, then north to Boston again, then back to Dallas where it finally stayed. Mrs. Dawkins and Jim Bill dropped by later that evening. Reba was overjoyed to see my folks, especially since she now had a sick husband on her hands. Mr. Dawkins had gone to the doctor that morning and had indeed contracted pneumonia. He would be in bed for at least two weeks.

Nancy and I took Jim Bill to her bedroom which by now had been pieced back together. Thick cardboard had been placed over the lower half of the window. We pulled back the corner of the cardboard and showed Jim Bill the cut in the screen where the shadow had tried to get in. She described to him how Dottie had attacked the shadow, where the struggle had been and which way the man had fled. Jim Bill had always taken animals for granted but later that evening, when he thought Nancy and I weren't watching, he called Dottie to him, pet her and even gave her a hug. "Mighty fine dog," he said to her under his breath. "Hope some day to get me a dog like you." It was the first compliment either of us ever heard from Jim Bill about any animal, let alone our Dottie. The highest verbal honor any animal would ever have bestowed on it had been uttered from the lips of Jim Bill.

To our delight, LD was asked by Daddy to stay with us for another few days. Her shoulder and hip were sore from the fall, and it was all she could do to raise her right arm. Mama or Daddy worked her into our family as though she was part of it. She spent most of the next few days entertaining us. We taught her how to play Parcheesi, and she taught us how to play Dominoes. At night, while Mama and Daddy were reading the newspaper on their screen porch, we three and sometimes Jim Bill would sit on our back porch taking in the evening.

"Do you think he'll come back?" Nancy asked LD one night, looking up at her from her lap.

"Don't rightly know, honey," she answered. "I suspect if'n I was him I'd steer clear of this house for a good time to come. Lordy, that dog would o' been e'nuff to scare tarnation outta me. If he's got any mind at all, he'll leave this place alone and go on 'bout his bizness."

"That's good," Nancy answered. A long silence came next.

"You have a family, LD?" I asked.

"Not any more, baby. Used to, though. My Papa died just after I was born and my Mama, well, she passed away nigh five winters ago. I had a little boy—the pride of my life he was, and I loved him so very much, just like your Mama and Papa love the both of you. Sometimes it seems having him with me was like a dream, like somethin' that happened a long, long time ago. Then other times it seems I was holdin' him on my lap just yesterday and talking to him and pressing his small, little body next to mine."

"That makes me sad, LD," Nancy sighed. "What did you call him? What was his name?"

"Why, Jonathan, princess. I called him Jonathan. I had always liked that name. It always seemed to call to mind for me things that were soft and warm and gentle. Indeed, princess, he was that," she sighed.

"Where is he now? What happened to him?"

"Maybe LD doesn't want to talk about it," Nancy said looking at me. "You don't have to if you don't want to, LD."

"It's fine, honey," she answered. "Talkin' 'bout it helps me with it. He's dead now, honey. It was poison that killed him, when I wasn't lookin'. He drank some lye when my back was to him. At first I didn't know what the matter was. Then I saw the lye bottle next to him and knew right away. There wasn't nothin' I could do. I tried, though. Lord knows I tried. I watered the inside of his throat as best I could for as long as I could but it didn't help none. He barely could get a breath I had so much water goin' into him. The doctor, he finally came and just looked at me and shook his head. By the time he had gotten there it was too late. The lye'd burned his poor, tiny throat so bad, so terrible bad. I took him in my arms and helt him close. It seemed like for all eternity. His crying got lower and lower. Then nothin' at all. I kept rocking' him though, back and forth, back and forth long after I knew he'd left me. I just couldn't let him go." LD wiped her eyes.

"But I still have a son," she continued," 'cause at times I can still feel him with me. A sudden little wind'll blow or I'll feel something tiny fluttering around me and I'll know it's him. Sometimes I picture Jonathan floating with the blue sky and the clouds, free like a bird and singing just as pretty. I'll look up and think I see him in one of those soft, little cotton-like clouds that linger awhile. I think maybe that's his way of tellin' me he's still with his Mama, lookin' and watchin' over me in his own sweet and special way."

The moon that July night was full and softly bright. We stared at it as the conversation fell into a type of reverent silence. Almost miraculously, a small white cloud floated against the face of the moon.

"Look, LD!" Nancy said pointing to it. "Look up there. There's Jonathan!"

LD raised her eyes. Tears were running down her cheeks. Suddenly, she smiled

"Praise Jesus," she whispered. "Praise Him and thank Him!"

It was not until many years later that we would learn that Mama and Daddy had asked LD, in private, to stay with our family. She had tearfully declined their invitation. When we asked our parents LD's reason for leaving, they were at a loss. "Reasons she chose not to explain", was all Daddy said. "All we could do was offer." Before she left, we found a thousand Jonathans for LD.

Jim Bill was the best, Nancy came in second and I ended up third. LD would separate them for us—the ones that looked like she'd pictured Jonathan from the ones that didn't. One cloud was too big, the other too small, the other too white, the last too dark.

"You see him when you least expect it", LD said. "You'll feel him when he comes."

What the old cottonwood taught us about wisdom and understanding, LD taught us about human tragedy and faith. It was one of the many lessons Nancy and I would stow away in our memories and in our hearts as our lives unfolded on 1854 Garrett Street.

Two days later, we all walked LD to the bus stop. She boarded the bus, walked to its back and sat down. She waived to us from inside and threw us a kiss. The bus pulled away in a cloud of black smoke and grew smaller and smaller as it belched its way down Fitzhugh Avenue. Dottie whimpered and Nancy and I cried. The bus that had once brought Daddy home to us had now taken our LD away.

That night felt like a bad dream. The back porch was empty and the sounds of the darkness mirrored our mood. Dottie was sullen and withdrawn, and even Jim Bill seemed depressed. Mama and Daddy loitered in the kitchen for awhile, called half-heartedly to us two or three times, then finally gave up and left. The back door slammed, the kitchen light went off and Jim Bill, Nancy, Dottie and I were left alone—like LD.

CHAPTER 12

The absence of LD and the continuance of unbearable heat prolonged the July summer days. Days became longer and more tedious, broken only by the depressing prospect of school for Nancy and perhaps also for me.

Sheriff Wade had dropped by on several occasions to see how things were going. As I look back now, he was a sincere man who was unfortunately weighed down by his office, his stomach and even his gun. His uniform was always wrinkled and unkept as he peered at us from sun-scorched, half-closed eyes. Sheriff Wade's revolver hung loosely holstered at his right side and, despite his constant readjustment, kept wriggling its way over his protruding belly towards the floor. He was a strange contradiction to the western heroes we had seen on television—Hop-a-long Cassidy, Gene Autry and Bob Steel.

Dottie had been diagnosed as having worms some weeks before, and Jim Bill, Nancy and I were in the process of trying to find them. We were exasperated. We checked her mouth, her ears, her fur and even her drool-spit. We found nothing.

"Must be a foul diagnosis," Jim Bill concluded. "She ain't got no signs of them worm things. Nothing crawling that I can see. The doctors make mistakes sometimes," he said. "They did that with my Aunt Mable. Said she had a tape worm and when they finally opened her up weren't no worm at all—just some shiny thing that kept her from going, if you know what I mean. Jim Bill's diagnosis was soon left behind when we were called by Mama and Daddy to come in.

"Sheriff Wade again—just wait and see," Nancy remarked. "I hate that man! "He ruins all of our fun."

This Saturday afternoon had not been his best day as evidenced by the dark wet spots under his armpits. He smelled hot and sweaty. His occasional grin always exposed two gaps in his side teeth, and, each time he pronounced the letter "s", the air passing through his teeth produced a subtle whistle which to Nancy and I seemed strangely remarkable. Were it not for the familiar Mexican hat he was holding in his hand, we wouldn't have taken him any more seriously than a lightning bug in a jar.

Nancy reacted.

"You've seen this hat before, honey?"

"Answer him, Nancy." Mama said.

Nancy nodded. "It looks like the one Mr. Ortiz wears." Dottie went up to it, sniffed it, then wagged her tail.

"Dottie knows it too," Nancy said. "It is his, isn't it? What's happened to him? Is he hurt?"

"No, honey," Wade answered. There was a long silence.

"Maybe we'd best take this up at another time," Wade said looking at Daddy.

"He's dead, isn't he?" Nancy blurted out suddenly.

"Nancy!" Mama shouted.

"He's dead—I know he is! That's his hat. He'd never leave it behind or lose it! Outside of Jasper, it was the one thing he loved the most. And Jasper! What about Jasper?"

She glared at the Sheriff. He looked back at her, nervously adjusted his gunbelt, then bowed his head a bit. He didn't have to answer her—she knew. Tears filled her eyes. She stormed out of the living room in a hysterical frenzy. Nancy ran to her room and slammed the door behind her.

Daddy peered at the Sheriff while Mama slowly sunk to a sitting position on the edge of the couch. The full impact of what Nancy had said had just sunken in.

"Is that true, Wade? Is she right?"

"Yes, sir. One of my deputies found him this morning. He was a mess. Whoever done it wasn't much kinder to his mule. Looked like it was done with an axe or maybe even by a real strong man with a butcher knife. We'll be able to figure out more once the coroner gets back with us."

"But why are you here? Surely you don't think we had anything to do with it?

"No, Sir! But my deputy found a note the person left at the scene. It was pinned to Ortiz's hat real careful like so as not to get any blood on it."

"So?"

"You look at it, sir. Tell me what you think. The writin' look familiar?"

"Jesus Christ," Daddy whispered. "The writing looks like the same as Nancy's note."

"It ain't easy to tell, and I ain't trying to alarm you but this word—this 'un right there. Looks like it could be your daughter's name. This guy wasn't too good at learnin' proper letter formation was he?"

"I can't make out the writing but if I were to guess, it seems like that might be Nancy's name."

Daddy handed the note to Mama. Her hands were shaking as she took it from him.

"So you're saying, Sheriff, that whoever killed Ortiz is probably the same person who is stalking our daughter? If that's the case…" Daddy turned and walked to the window. "Do you have any idea who this person might be?"

"We're following up on some leads but as far as we make out right now, nobody saw nothin' or heard nothin'. Best we can tell is that it happened within the last couple of days, within the same time frame you had your break in a while back."

Daddy nodded.

"Could just be coincidence, but if'n it was my daughter I'd sure take care—just to be on the right side of safe," Wade said walking slowly to the door. "If this someone is after her, he's a mighty peculiar dog. He must want her real bad to have killed a worn-out old Mexican. About took his head clean off. It wasn't just one cut, sir, but alot of them—like he was real mad. He's a sick man. Them kind gets jealous real easy like. Could be he thought Ortiz was messing with her or maybe he was thinking that the Mexican was infringin' on what he thought was his property. She's young and cute—feisty to boot—the kind that can get under the skin of a man like this and stay there. Ain't her fault or yours for that matter. Just the way some people are."

"She is in danger," Daddy concluded out loud.

"Danger is a mighty peculiar word, Sir. If she was my daughter, I'd sure take care.

Looks like she's got someone after her who wants her real bad. My professional opinion," Wade added as he went out the screen door "is that we've got a problem on our hands. I'd be lying if I told you different."

"So what do we do now?" Daddy asked.

"Sit tight and keep her close," Wade answered. "Keep a look out and tell your neighbors to do the same 'til we can get to the bottom of this. I'll have the boys at the Department put this as a priority. In the meantime I'd appreciate your calling me at your convenience so we can sit a spell and talk about the situation. Might just be coincidence for all we know. I'll keep you posted. You do the same for me." Wade tipped his Stetson and waddled out the door.

Shortly after his departure, Nancy came out of her room and went to the back porch. I went with her, and we sat for a long time, not saying a word. We watched as the daylight silently and relentlessly dried up. Dottie joined us and finally Jim Bill. The locusts' drone became louder and louder as the day's waning summer light finally faded, ray by ray to complete darkness.

"I've heard about Sheriff Wade," Jim Bill eventually said. "He ain't much to look at but the Herald says he's powerful good. Here tell he's the best investigator the city has. He investigated that fire in Casa View and said it weren't set by nobody else but the owner—trying to get some insurance money. I'd be honored if he was calling on me."

Nancy stirred.

"He solved that crazy case 'bout the chicken coop murderer. Caught him red handed with his axe and his victim's head in a bag—if my memory serves me correctly. Papers wouldn't picture it though. They said it was too gruesome."

Nancy motioned for Dottie. Dottie came and lay down beside her. They were both exhausted and confused. Neither of them had noticed the silence or the heat. Panting as though she would die, Dottie stayed next to Nancy until the moon came up. She barked twice at something in the backyard and sent us all flying into the house. The second time Daddy came out with his twenty-two and shooed all of us inside. He wandered around the back yard, flashlight and pistol in hand, mumbling something under his breath. We saw a streak of light, then saw a flash and heard the pistol go off. He fell, then laid there until Mama came flying to him. She took the gun, and helped him inside. "He's fine," Mama said. "Just drunk. Help me to bed with him."

We followed Mama inside and helped her put Daddy to bed. He talked about this and that then finally passed out when his head hit the pillow.

"Go on out now, you three. The excitement's over" she whispered. "It will all be fine in the morning."

For once Mama was wrong. Within fifteen minutes after Daddy's gun went off, at least ten of the neighbors came running to our rescue—their shotguns and pistols loaded and pointing every which way. "It's nice to know," Mama finally told them, "that you're thinking about us. The only one who could have been killed tonight was my husband. We're all safe, and we thank you for coming."

"Anytime, Ma'am!" a shadow named Mr. Dawkins said from the yard. "Just anytime at all." Then as fast as they came, the men of the night were gone.

Looking back, the silence of that night was both a blessing and a curse. Jim Bill had long since gone home and our inside lights had finally dimmed. "Oh!" Nancy cried out in the middle of the night, and from a sleepy mist there came Mama's comforting "Go to sleep." I heard LD yelling out for Jonathan once again and saw her raise her hands in glory to the clouds. The night was calm and the drone of our air-cooling unit told us the soul of the Texas summer heat was settled in. Dottie barked at some strange sounds known only to her—a stray cat or maybe an opossum, I thought. She barked into the wee hours of the morning. She was telling us something was wrong. Nancy was too tired and didn't wake up and Daddy, well, he was still passed out. I sat halfway up in bed and called Dottie to me. It was the strangest sound either of us had ever heard. It was Mama crying.

The hours crawled relentlessly by, then the days and finally a week or two. Nancy confined herself to the house and refused to leave the yard. Mama acted as though she didn't mind at all and tried to include Nancy in some of the more pleasant chores around the house. Nancy would begin them but not long after would drift away from them. We knew something was on her mind. Mama tried talking to her, to reassure her that nothing else would happen. But Nancy was suspect. Even though Mama and Daddy hadn't told her she was in any immediate danger, she was smart and could tell something wasn't quite right. The more Mama reassured her, the more withdrawn she became.

We were a sight to behold during these few weeks. The doorbell and telephone became antagonists, and, as for Daddy, everyone who he didn't know became a suspect. The milkman was suspect, the mailman was suspect and so was even the blue jay on the windowsill. He had quit drinking, which, to Nancy, proved something was amiss. When she confronted Mama with this conclusion, Mama smiled and simply said, "Your father decided to go on a diet."

The situation became even more aggravating for Daddy when the drone of the air cooler suddenly stopped one night after supper. He checked it as best he could and finally threw up his hands. "Damn thing!" he said as he stomped out of the kitchen, wiping the sweat off his forehead. "Just when you need the bastard the most!" It was the last Monday of July, and he knew summer was far from over. The Titche's repairman was out the first thing the next morning, and he wasted no time confirming Daddy's suspicions. The water cooler would need to be totally replaced. He told Mama it couldn't "rightfully be done 'fore two days."

The next day, the house was like a slow-bake oven—so much so that we all decided we preferred sweltering outside to inside—at least there was a hot breeze. "Now I know how those Thanksgiving turkeys feel," Jim Bill said hosing himself off. Mama lunged at him and grabbed the hose.

"You'd better run!" she yelled. She got me first, then Jim Bill, then Nancy and finally even Dottie. We were dripping from head to toe. Jim Bill wrestled the hose from Mama and threw it to Nancy.

"Git her!" he yelled at Nancy. "Git her good!" Nancy looked, then quick as a cat turned it on Mama. Mama raced around the backyard laughing and hollering for the longest time. She finally flung up her dripping hands and cried "Stop! That's enough!" Nancy sprayed her a few more seconds then finally quit. Our first water fight had ended. As we were walking towards the back, Mama took Nancy's chin in her hand and looked at her. "Keep smiling. It looks good."

Mama convinced Daddy when he got home that night to have the new water cooler put in the next day. Daddy later told us it was the house's heat that made him get the new cooler so fast—but we knew different. Whatever the case, by noon the monotonous drone of the new water cooler could be heard. We spent all afternoon seated under it, watching and admiring it.

A few days later Daddy came home from work all smiles. He seemed both happy and relieved. He hugged Mama and me, then picked up Nancy in his arms. "Honey," he announced, "no need to worry anymore. Sheriff Wade called today. They caught the guy!"

Mr. Dawkins, Reba and Jim Bill were the first ones to our sides when they heard the good news. Mr. and Mrs. Savoy dropped by and almost every one of our neighbors brought some type of food or desserts, as though it were a funeral rather than a celebration. The good news had spread awfully fast.

Daddy and Mama soon set up our portable fans to keep the air moving. The wind they created sent the napkins we had set out flying every which way and blew the paper cups off the table onto the floor. Their presence was everyone's outward sign of relief. Nancy was safe. We were safe. They were safe. Finally Daddy thanked them for their help and support and ushered them out gracefully. We saw Mama take Daddy in his arms after they had left and heard him cry. Sensing something was wrong, Dottie went to him. He hugged her too then he called for Nancy and me.

Daddy's eyes were blood-shot, and his face drooped. The humidity of the day and night sent his usually combed hair into a split-end frenzy. It looked as though he was two inches taller. He hugged us both, tried to say something then declined to say it. "Go on to bed," he finally uttered. The roar of our attic fan that evening broke the sweltering heat of past nights. The windows we had shut for weeks were thrown open. That night the fan was like an inverted tornado—it sucked up all of our fears and anxieties and threw them out of our house. They landed somewhere on our side yard, but, like the

Johnson grass that always managed to survive, refused to wither away.

Except for the newspaper article that reminded us of Mr. Ortiz and Jasper, Mama and Daddy did all they could to distance us from the murder and murderer who Wade swore committed it. The police had requested Nancy be brought downtown to identify the man they had arrested. Daddy told them she had never actually seen the man and that such a procedure would be pointless. He had previously asked Nancy in a round about way if she had seen the man. She said it had been too dark. LD's name had been brought up on several occasions but was finally dismissed.

"Oh, well," Wade said after one of his drop-bys. "Don't really matter anyway since we're trying him for murder not breakin' and enterin'. We got the goods on 'em. No need for y'all to worry no more."

The man Sheriff Wade had arrested was named Homer Boggs. Accordingly to the Sheriff, he was a drifter, a down-and-outer, with a long record of misdemeanors and other petty crimes. He walked with a limp, and the police had confiscated a switchblade that had the same blood type as Ortiz's on it when they arrested him. He was charged with murder and locked up tight in the city jail. Wade said that despite the hours of questioning that Boggs had endured, he had never admitted either killing Ortiz, leaving notes for Nancy or robbing any house let alone ours. "Don't amount to much anyway," Wade commented. "He ain't never admitted to any of the lesser crimes he's done in the past. Didn't figure he'd admit to the one that'll send him to the chair. He's the man," Wade kept reassuring Mama and Daddy. "Don't suspect you or your little 'un will have no more trouble from the likes of this guy. Consider it all as a thing of the past."

Wade's assessment of the situation that had been hanging over our heads was both comforting and welcomed. The fact that Boggs would be tried for murder instead of breaking and entering freed Nancy of any possibility of having to testify at all. It was the perfect outcome to the whole situation, and we were all relieved.

Slowly but surely, life at 1854 Garrett Street returned to normal. Nancy and Jim Bill went back to their Shakespeare play-acting, and the summer twilights found the three of us running to and fro with jars lit up as though they were moving lamplights. They pulsated a glowing gold from the lightning bugs we had caught and put inside them.

One evening Warren Culbertson, the Channel 4 weatherman, introduced us to Beulah. She was a hurricane and was headed into the Gulf of Mexico. He talked optimistically of rain and cooler temperatures for us, if Beulah stayed on her current course.

"What's that thing in the middle of the hurricane," Nancy asked one night as we were watching. "That hole."

"That's the eye of the hurricane," Mama answered. "It's very deceiving. Inside the eye everything is calm and peaceful, but outside the eye everything's the exact opposite. The eye makes people think the storm is over with, but, just as they let down their guard, here it all comes again, this time from the opposite direction and even worse. Things can be deceiving at times," she concluded.

"That's why you never leave your guard down," Daddy added.

Neither Nancy nor I understood Daddy's comment, and we both dismissed it like so many of his other comments we hadn't understood previously. Looking back, our situation, though seemingly resolved, was a lot like Beulah. We were unaware that we were in the eye of our own personal hurricane. The relief we were experiencing was but a respite from what was to come.

CHAPTER 13

Without LD, Jaspar and Mr. Ortiz, the days on Garrett Street became long and monotonous. Whatever relief Mr. Culbertson and his Beulah promised soon fizzled. The storm's track took it hundreds of miles north and east of us. Jim Bill and Nancy had long since run out of Shakespeare lines. Nancy complained she was too hot and tired to learn any more and that her acting days were officially over until fall.

Our neighborhood, like everyone else's, was withering under the continuous heat. There was nothing that could be done to escape it. Our city fathers become even more alarmed with water shortage problems, and they soon turned to White Rock Lake to bail them out. New city ordinances forbidding the use of water for this and for that appeared daily in "The Herald". Lawns and flowerbeds that had once been lush and green turned brown and barren. The ground cracked. House foundations buckled. Wood frames shrunk and peeled under the incessant summer onslaught.

"Eighteen days of 100 plus temperatures," Mr. Culbertson said, "and no end in sight."

Nancy, Jim Bill and I, when he could, took up sleeping on our back porch. It faced south and thus was treated occasionally to a light southwesterly breeze. Jim Bill complained it "weren't no breeze at all. Just air them mosquitoes flying by him made" as he lay there trying to sleep.

The stagnant, night air hung heavily on those warm summer nights as did our imaginations. We would wonder out loud about the Lady of the Lake and plan a fantasy trip to White Rock to see her. Jim Bill concluded that this is what had to be done since our house was too far from her haunting territory. "One of these days," he announced half asleep," we ought to go." It was a trip to White Rock we took each night without ever leaving Garrett Street. We'd be walking along the dark shores through the blinding rain and blowing wind. Then out of nowhere she'd appear, dressed in white and drenched to the skin. Jim Bill said she probably looked a lot like Nancy with her dark hair and deep brown eyes. In my mind, she had golden hair that stretched to her waste that blew behind her in the wind. Nancy would see her motioning for us to follow, but, despite my and Jim Bill's pleadings, Nancy wouldn't let us go. Then Mr. Savoy would appear, and the lady would get into his car and leave until we called her back the following night. To us the Lady of the Lake always accommodated our imaginations. Like Jonathan in the clouds, she was always there at our beck and call.

It was a deep Tuesday night in the third week of August, right after summer had moved just beyond its peak. Looking closely, you could see the sun going down in a little different spot from the previous day. The big and little dippers had already started their winter's journey to the west. The locusts and crickets hadn't noticed. They thought they were going to live forever. This night, though, a strange and different glow was hanging right above the horizon long after the sun had gone down. It was eerie and unfamiliar. Half asleep, I heard the phone ring. It sounded like the bells at Mass—three rings, then stop. Then three more rings, then stop. The lights came on in our house. It was the phone. Daddy answered it, and we heard him shout "Jesus!" He came running to us on the porch.

"The Dawkins' chicken coop is on fire!" he yelled. "You three stay here!"

We sprang to our feet and looked for Jim Bill. His pallet was empty. He knew.

"He's already there!" Nancy screamed. "Oh, Jim Bill!" Dottie ran after us. The sky behind the Dawkins' house was lit up. People were scurrying everywhere, swearing and hurling verbal commands at each other. Someone screamed "The Fire Department's on its way! They'll be here soon!"

"Get out of the way, you kids!" yelled a man as he ran by us. He was pulling a long snake hose behind him. "Spray the yards!" he yelled. Mama came running from inside the Dawkins' house with a bucket full of water. Daddy grabbed it and threw its contents on the loudly crackling fire which by now had engulfed the chicken coop. "Get some more!" he yelled at Mama. "Lots more!"

The panicking neighbors next door to the Dawkins were frantically trying to hose down what was left of their bone-dry yard. The fire exploded several times, each time spewing a fountain of red-hot sparks and embers skyward. We peered through the chaotic mass of scurrying bodies trying to see Jim Bill. He was nowhere to be found.

Our search for Jim Bill lead us to the front yard of the Dawkins' where in the distance we could hear the bells and sirens of the approaching fire engines. They turned off Fitzhugh onto Garrett, their red and white blinking lights getting brighter and their frenzied sirens and bells becoming almost deafening. Only Nancy heard the yelp. Her face immediately twisted with pain and disbelief. She ran to the street and screamed. There was Dottie.

"Oh no! No! Get Daddy!" she screamed. "Get Daddy" she screamed again pushing me towards the fire. "Hurry!"

"I'm not leaving you or Dottie!" I yelled.

"Oh, Dottie," Nancy said bending down over her. Dottie's tale wagged a bit.

"Go get Daddy now!" she screamed at me again.

"I'm not leaving either of you," I mumbled back.

From out of nowhere a figure approached. It was walking towards us then, as though it knew the situation, began running to us. It was Jim Bill.

"Oh, Jim Bill," Nancy said. "Dottie's been run over. She's dying!"

Jim Bill reached down and patted Dottie. "She's in mighty poor shape. We've got to move her out of the road. I'll have to carry her. Hope she don't bite me."

Jim Bill reached down and gently picked up Dottie. As he carried her she began licking his face. "You'll be all right, girl," Jim Bill kept telling her. "You'll be fine." He placed her on the grass next to the curb.

"Go get your daddy, Nancy. Tell him to come quick!"

Nancy broke and ran, and I started to cry. "She'll be all right—right Jim Bill?" He didn't say anything. "Go get me some towels. We got to stop her bleeding."

I ran inside our house and grabbed as many towels as I could carry. When I got back to Jim Bill's side he yanked them from me. "Easy now, girl," His voice quivered. "Easy does it."

Dottie's eyes were wide open as though she didn't understand what was happening. She tried to get up once but Jim Bill coaxed her back down. Her drool spit was foamed and tinged with red. Her chest heaved with each breath.

"Maybe a little water will help her," I said. Jim Bill nodded.

"Better hurry," he answered.

When I arrived back Jim Bill was patting Dottie. He and she were alone. The blinking lights dimmed; the light of the fire disappeared; the human commotion seemed far away. The water I was carrying in Dottie's dish didn't matter anymore.

Jim Bill kept whispering to her in words only he and she could hear. He looked up at me and shook his head.

"What did you tell her!" I yelled at Jim Bill. "What did you say?"

He looked up at me. His eyes were ablaze. "She felt you must not of loved her no more—takin' your time with the water and all."

Jim Bill was upset, but I was crushed. I had gotten the water as fast as I could but it wasn't fast enough. Tears welled up in my eyes, and I looked dumbfounded at Jim Bill. He took her head and gently rested it on the grass. He stroked her once as a lonely tear worked it's way down his cheek. That was his good-bye.

We buried Dottie that night in our backyard. The waning light from the Dawkins chicken-coop fire underlined the finality of the night's events. The Dawkins had lost their coop, but we had lost our Dottie. Daddy groaned; Mama tried to tend to Nancy. Jim Bill and I sat silently on the back porch. He finally got up and left without saying a word. The loneliness of the night and its sounds scared me. From habit, I called for Dottie. She couldn't come.

I heard the sounds of Nancy breathing as I walked passed her bedroom. She was asleep. It was dawning outside, and an empty feeling came over me. I didn't want to be alone. I crawled in next to her. That is when I noticed it. On her bedstead was a shadowy piece of dirty, folded paper. Scribbled on its face was the name "Nancy". I recognized the writing. We had all seen it before.

CHAPTER 14

I can imagine how Daddy felt coming home from his day's work after the night we had just experienced. The temperature on our gage read 103. Jim Bill, Nancy and me were fighting with the Shouts'.

Daddy broke us up and sent the Shouts home. "They made fun of Jim Bill's cross for Dottie," Nancy explained to Daddy. "Mama said it was okay to fight them."

"They're mad, sir that Dottie chased their dogs away from Jasper. They aren't no matter, sir," Jim Bill explained. "This here cross is the main thing. I made it for Dottie from the chicken coop wood. It's burnt a little but it's a mighty fine marker."

Jim Bill's marker had Jim Bill written all over it. The ends of the cross section boasted a hook for Dottie's collar and another hook on its opposite end for her tags. Her bowl was the top hat. Finally Jim Bill had carved "Our Friend" across its vertical plank.

The second burial for Dottie occurred within a few minutes after Daddy arrived home. It was less traumatic than the first. Nancy was there this time as was Mama and Daddy and me and, of course, Jim Bill with his marker. Nancy and Mama had brought some holy water and sprinkled it on her grave. We all went through our liturgy of what she meant to each of us. Like LD's leaving, yesterday's joys had paved the way for today's sorrows.

Mama made a comment that sometimes family animals die at the worst times—when everything is in chaos. "Their dying helps remind us of how good things used to be and how we ought to appreciate what we have while we have it." she reasoned. None of us really understood Mama's comment, nor did we ask her to explain. Jim Bill asked permission to place his marker on Dottie's grave. He walked up, then went to Nancy. He handed it to her.

"You do it," he said. "Here's my good kerchef so's you can dry your eyes."

Nancy took the marker and tried to hammer it in. The ground was too cracked and hard. She let it drop to the ground.

"Jim Bill and I will do it tomorrow," I said. "I'll keep it with me tonight."

"No need to do that," came a vaguely familiar voice. "That dog was a great animal! I'll have one of my deputies sink it tomorrow." It was Sheriff Wade. He had dropped by again.

Sheriff Wade had the knack of dropping by at the worst times imaginable. This was but one example. His visits were strictly updates according to him, but they always caught us unprepared and with our minds on something else. There was never a phone call or a warning. He'd just show up and begin commenting.

His interruption of Dottie's formal-burial was aggravating to all of us. Jim Bill pulled away and eventually left, as did Nancy. Daddy tried to coax them to stay but they refused.

"From now on call before you come," Daddy said to Wade.

"What for? Just in the neighborhood and figured I'd swing by to tell you the latest developments—'less, of course, you don't care to know."

Daddy wiped the sweat from his forehead. "Give us a minute, if you don't mind."

Daddy, Mama and I were the only ones left to tell Dottie goodbye. Daddy marked the grave by placing Jim Bill's marker on the ground beside it.

"Can set that for you tomorrow, if you want." Wade offered again. "My deputy can do it quick as a flash. It'll last too."

"Maybe," Daddy answered. "I'll let you know."

"We're about to get a confession out of Boggs about Ortiz," Wade said drawing Daddy aside as though we had just buried a doodlebug, "but we ain't quite there yet. If he confesses, he's goin' to the pen for sure—maybe even the chair. He knows it too. That's what I think's holding him up. We'll get it eventually." Wade's eyes squinted as he looked into the sun. "Only thing," Wade continued, "Boggs still ain't sain anything about your house or your daughter or anything else relatin' to your personal case. That scares me a bit."

"You said he was the one!"

"I ain't saying he isn't the one. I'm just sayin' he ain't confessed to anything as yet. We've asked him directly a number of times. He just about owns up to everything but that." Wade took of his hat and wiped his face with his red kerchief. "I saw Boggs today. He's a mighty broken man, sir—plum down and out. Guard says he climbs the walls at night and talks to himself all day. Don't rightly know, but if he was the one, seems to me he wouldn't of minded ownin' 'up to everythin'."

"Nancy's still in danger." Daddy concluded.

Wade nodded. "Seems so."

Dottie's grave was set in concrete the following evening like Wade said it would be. Despite Mama's protests, Officer Bradley kept on doing his work. "Orders, ma'am," he said. "I've got orders to do this here." Mama grabbed the shovel from his hands and told him to leave. He seemed shocked and confused.

"I don't like doin' this anymore than you like me doin' it, ma'am. It's hot and ma back is killin' me! I ain't even begun the concrete yet. Sheriff Wade told me to get out here and git this done. Just obeyin' orders, ma'am. Hope you understand."

Mama nodded and smiled. "Nancy, get this officer some lemonade." She held out his shovel to him.

The man said his name was Jim Bradley. He was thirty-four years old. He was tall and lanky and disappointed with this assignment. He had joined the police force to catch robbers and thieves and here he was "diggin' some grave for a poor ol' dog."

We soon found out Jim loved lemonade. The more he drank, the more he talked. He had a dog once, but it died when he was sixteen. Someone shot it, he said—never found out who. This assignment came hard for him. He hated burying pets, especially dogs, but strangely enough liked putting up markers for them. He had done it for his own dog. He said he cried so hard when he lost Dandelion, he's never cried since. Jim Bill showed him Dottie's special tombstone and the policeman thought it was a sight to behold. His eyes lit up.

"An East Texas dog burial—tags, and everythin'," he commented. Jim bill nodded. "Even a bowl for its top. Mighty fine, son." Jim Bill blushed.

"What was his name?"

"Dottie," Nancy said, approaching Officer Garrett. "She was a lady."

"Dottie," he said, stroking his chin. "Was she a shepherd?"

"A boxer," I answered. "She's saved our lives more than once. She was run over by the fire engines last night during the Dawkins's fire. We were just trying to say good-bye when Sheriff Wade came last night. He doesn't like dogs."

Bradley nodded as though he understood. "Wait a second," he said. "Let me get somethin' from my car."

By the time Officer Bradley returned Mama and Daddy had joined us "This here's a flare," he said. "Only supposed to burn it for emergencies since it's so dry. Help me dig this hole like my orders say and we'll burn it like a torch next to her grave. It'll light up the heavens and tell everyone how much Dottie meant to you."

We all joined in, even Daddy. Officer Bradley helped us all dig but ended up doing most of it himself. He talked and talked about his dog and said he wished he had some flares when he buried Dandelion.

Dottie went out that night in a hale of pink smoke, body-sweat and dirty hands. But she had her headstone. We celebrated her leaving us with another pitcher of lemonade. Officer Bradley set the flare in the right spot so we could all see Dottie's tombstone lit up.

"Bradley," Daddy said. "Thank you for your help."

"Thank you," he answered back, "for makin' this job a little easier for me." He finally climbed into his squad car and left.

Dottie's grave marker was like our water cooler—always there and always a reminder. When we walked out the back door, we'd see it. When we carried the trash to the alley, we'd see it, too. The small inscription Jim Bill had carved on the marker crosspiece said it all. She would always be our friend.

Officer Bradley was like so many of the other images we experienced on Garrett Street. He was there for a functional moment, then, like LD's Jonathan, disappeared like the clouds. Daddy called the Police Department several days later to thank Officer Bradley again for his help. The Sergeant said Bradley had resigned after his last assignment. He had left no forwarding address.

Looking back, Officer Bradley is another phantom, a type of mental mirage of times gone by. Nancy barely recognizes his name today. To justify my own memory, I sometimes go by Garrett Street to view our Dottie's plot. Occasionally I'll see a small cluster of disarrayed flower cuff lying beside her headstone, as if they had decided to stop there on purpose. They'd stay for awhile, paying their respects, then blow on to their next destination, as if on a predetermined schedule.

CHAPTER 15

After Dottie died, things at 1854 Garrett changed. The weather was still hot and oppressing—that's the only thing that seemed to remain the same. The Dawkins coop burned down to the ground and two other houses beside it met the same fate. The Fire Department said it was arson for sure, and they were looking hot and heavy for the person who started it.

The Fire Chief came to our house and asked Mama and Daddy all sorts of questions—where they were when it started and did they know where we were, too. Mr. Dawkins, for some reason, said he had seen Nancy and me near the coop right before the fire tore through it. Nancy, Jim Bill and I denied it to the Fire Chief's face. Despite his skepticism, Reba, Mama and Daddy believed us and sent him on his way. Mrs. Dawkins must have talked to Mr. Dawkins about it because it never came up again—not that it could have.

Mr. Dawkins' health had gotten worse. The frenzy of the fire depleted what energy he had left. Jim Bill wasn't the only one worrying about his father. The several weeks that followed were marked by a constant trail of meals and night vigils. Mama brought Mrs. Dawkins a novena, but Mrs. Dawkins, being Baptist, didn't know what to do with it. It finally ended with Mr. Dawkins' last, gasping breath shortly after midnight one night. Mama spent that night with Mrs.

Dawkins and the next day helped her prepare the funeral ceremonies. Jim Bill spent the night with us.

The three of us went to the back porch. Jim Bill was quiet and inside himself. His eyes would well with tears, and then he would wipe them. Then they'd well up again. The twilight of the day set the tone for Nancy. She went to Jim Bill and hugged him and cried. We had lost our dog, but Jim Bill had lost his Daddy.

"Oh, Jim Bill," Nancy would say.

The funeral was two days later. Being Catholics, we weren't supposed to attend, but all of my family did. Daddy skipped work to be there. We saw Mrs. Dawkins and Jim Bill walk out before the congregation and then sit down. The organ started playing, and the preacher began talking. I don't remember what he said. I remember Jim Bill helping his Mama. Daddy was somber and walked beside them in case they needed help. Mama dried her eyes with her hanky and supported Reba's other shoulder.

Nancy and I walked with Jim Bill up to his father's tented gravepit. He approached the deep hole with reluctant courage. Daddy came to help him, but Jim Bill said no. He motioned for Nancy and I to come next to him and together we dropped the hard, black sod on his father's coffin as they lowered the box into the ground.

Mr. Dawkins had been there when we were attacked. Today, I still see him sitting wide-eyed in our living room chair with his 12 gauge lying across his lap, protecting us from a shadowy figure that must have scared him too. The rains started the day he was buried, but no one except Jim Bill seemed to care. "Papa's got to be in heaven," Jim Bill commented to us shortly after the funeral when the three of us were alone. Nancy and I looked at him. We didn't know what to say.

"I just know he is—just as sure as my last name is Dawkins."

"How come, Jim Bill?"

"Well, listen. Cain't you hear it?"

We strained our ears as hard as we could but couldn't hear anything. We shook our heads at him.

"Can't hear anything," I finally admitted.

"That's just it," Jim Bill said smiling. "Daddy's still helping you. He's finally turned off your water cooler. He always said it was unhealthy."

CHAPTER 16

As usual Jim Bill was right plus some. Not only had Mr. Dawkins turned off our water cooler, but he had also turned on the overhead spicket. The three days following his funeral were marked by teeming rains and blustery south winds. Finally, an early cool front moved through and blew the clouds and rain away. Temperatures dropped to a tolerable level and the clean air and cool temperatures set everyone in a better mood—everybody except the Dawkins'.

Their house was closed and quiet. Even at night there was hardly a light to be seen in their parlor. The front door would open quickly then shut. Cars would drive up and then leave just as fast. Mama was the only one Reba would let in, and sometimes Daddy.

Nancy and I took affront to Jim Bill's snub and laid in the front yard after supper chasing the lightning bugs as they scurried to and fro. We even laid some bug-filled jars by Jim Bill's front door, but still he would not come out.

We asked Mama and Daddy about it, and they told us to leave Jim Bill and his Mama alone, to let them sort things out without people bothering them. Mama said Jim Bill was busy helping since he was the only man about the house now. Nonetheless, each afternoon during that setting summer we would continue to laugh and play in full view of the Dawkins'. We were sure Jim Bill would hear us and show up.

I finally, but reluctantly, decided to show the note I had found on the nightstand to Nancy. I had no idea what her response would be. To my surprise she wasn't so much scared as angry and upset. She realized this man had set fire to the coop so he could deliver his note to her without being seen. "He killed Dottie and Mr. Dawkins, too" she said to me that night right before bedtime. "I hope he goes right to the fires of hell and stays there!"

The next day was Saturday, and we spent the majority of the morning wondering about Jim Bill. Before, he would have come over by the time Winky Dink was over on television, but the morning dragged on and on and still there was no sign of him.

"Maybe he's sick," I commented to Nancy during lunch, but she shrugged the idea off.

"Maybe I'll just go knock on his door to see if he can come out." she thought out loud.

"Don't you dare," Mama told her as she handed us our milk. "Let them alone. You two can last a while longer without Jim Bill. I'm sure he'll come over when he's ready. Have a little patience. How would you feel if your Daddy had just died?"

"Daddy wouldn't do that to us," Nancy commented.

"Just the same," Mama said. "Let them be."

The Saturday morning we had looked forward to developed into an even more boring afternoon. Nancy was intent on getting the note into Jim Bill's hands one way or the other. She finally decided we needed to make him a come out package and attach the note to it. That way he would get it for sure.

"How are we going to get it to him?" I asked. "We haven't seen him in days."

Nancy thought for a minute. "We'll deliver it to him ourselves—tonight—at his window," she answered. "We'll wait until Mama and Daddy are asleep and sneak it over to him. It won't take long."

We spent the rest of the afternoon making Jim Bill's package. We packed up two of my ballbearing boulders, a quarter from the change Daddy left on his dresser and a lock of Dottie's hair. Nancy retrieved a pack of Charms from her hiding place and threw it in the box. We put the top on and taped the note to its outside so Jim Bill couldn't miss seeing it. "He'll know this is from us once he opens the box," Nancy concluded.

"How's he going to know to come out?"

"He's not stupid, you know. He'll see the note and understand we need him. How could he not?"

"Aren't you afraid the man will be out there? What if he is? Then what?"

"Yes, I'm scared," she answered. "But what else are we going to do? We'll just have to hope he isn't."

We waited until the last lights in our house were turned off then waited some more. We heard Daddy starting to snore and knew that was a good sign. He was finally dropping off into a deep sleep. Mama was a different story. She had always slept, as Daddy had once said, with one eye open. Unfortunately for us this night, her maternal instincts struck once again. We were no sooner out our window and headed across the street when we heard her.

"You two are in trouble," she said grabbing us by our pajama collars. "The idea! Wait until I tell your father. And what is this?" she said, grabbing our package. "Get to bed and don't let me see you out here again! The idea!"

Like whipped puppy dogs we followed Mama back into the house. We knew better than to say anything. It wouldn't have done much good. Mama sent us to our rooms. "Mama," Nancy finally said to Mama as she climbed into bed. "We miss Jim Bill."

"Nonsense," she replied. "Go to bed!"

I wondered what Daddy would do to us as I laid wide-eyed groping for answers. Mama had taken our package and our gifts for Jim Bill. We were caught red-handed defying them. We knew we would pay the price. The glimmer of my last hope died when Mama turned off the front room light a few minutes later. She had seen the package and read the note and even found Daddy's quarter.

The next day was Sunday and that meant Mass. Nancy and I were extra good during the service, but Mama purposely ignored us. We sat in our pew like fallen angels knowing we were guilty to the core. Bored, Daddy drew us to him then let us go. He had seen Mama's glance.

That Sunday afternoon, while we were lying under the cottonwood, Jim Bill came out. "Your Mama saved my life this afternoon," he said laying down beside us. "She's truly remarkable."

Jim Bill was right again, but we had no idea what Mama had done or what brought him to his conclusion. We would find out later that Mama had talked to Mrs. Dawkins after we had returned from Church and shown her the note. Mrs. Dawkins hugged Jim Bill shortly afterwards and shooed him outside. "Here's your quarter back," he said, handing the coin to Nancy. "I'll keep Dottie's hair, if you don't mind. And here's your boulders back too." he said pushing them towards me. "I ate the Charms."

Forces more mysterious than Superman's had been at work for us that day. Jim Bill was restored to us, and that was all that mattered at the time. The strange force that had been responsible for finally freeing Jim Bill we didn't acknowledge until sometime later. Its mysterious name was Mama.

CHAPTER 17

The serenity around our neighborhood lasted as long as our late-August cool spell. The Stewart's and the Long's houses across the street had been reduced to rubble by the fire, a fact we had all overlooked during all of the recent commotion. We had never known these families very well but seeing them sifting slowly through the ashes for what was left of their belongings made the impact of the last few weeks clear. These neighbors were the beneficiaries of a problem that wasn't even theirs. They'd pick through the rubble, then sift, then pick again. They'd save something here, then let something else go. Their lives lay before them in the ashes, and they were determined to retrieve as much of it as they could.

Mama and Daddy were affected by these neighbors' losses. They'd offer them dinner and water and whatever else they thought was needed, but their good intentions were always met with a genuine smile and a "No thanks. We'll make do."

Finally Mama and Daddy quit offering, and after several days the Longs and the Stewarts finally walked away from the ashes for good. Their loss had been devastating both for them and for us. It was a burden Daddy would carry with him to his grave. After he died I looked at his checkbook. He had been voluntarily paying both the Stewarts and the Longs fifty dollars per month in hopes it might compensate them for a part of their losses. These disbursements had taken place each month for almost thirty-five years.

Our neighbors' abandoned homes, like Dottie's grave, were a constant reminder of a once carefree life gone south. Even though Jim Bill's visits were more frequent, so were Sheriff Wade's. Daddy constantly questioned Wade about who it was, but Wade had no answers. "What am I supposed to do?" he finally asked Wade. Wade answered by shrugging his shoulders.

Nancy was nervous now—even at times scared. She would be attending Sacred Heart Elementary School the Monday after Labor Day. We were told this over a dinner of peas, carrots and pork chops which even the Sheriff declined due to an acidic stomach.

Sheriff Wade offered to pick her up and drive her home from school but Mama and Daddy eventually turned him down. They wanted Nancy's first days of school to be as normal as possible—despite the goings on around us. Daddy would drop her off each morning at the school, and the bus driver would bring her home when school was over. The bus driver would be informed of the situation, according to Wade. In Daddy's eyes, the plan was a good one—simple and direct. It left little margin for error.

Mama and Daddy's decision regarding Nancy's schooling had not been an easy one. Since its onset, Daddy became more and more frustrated with it. Wade had hinted earlier that postponing Nancy's entry into school until he had a better handle on the case might not be a bad idea. Mama, on the other hand, would have none of it. She said her daughter would arrive at school on time everyday, attend all day, and go home when she was supposed to. Their ifs, ands, and buts were silenced when Mama simply walked out of the room.

The frets and worries of the days' ordeals did little to upset our regular routines. Jim Bill came over as often as he used to—maybe even more—since Mrs. Dawkins has softened his chore-load a bit.

Mama and Daddy were a different story. Busted plumbing, car repairs and an assortment of other horribly timed maladies over which they had no control had drained their finances. What little savings they had left were soon eaten-up and Daddy, in particular, was feeling the worst of it. The final straw occurred when I overheard him telling Mama that he had just borrowed the last available monies from his life insurance policy to pay Nancy's first month tuition at Sacred Heart Elementary School. It was doubtful, he went on saying in much stronger terms, they could afford to send her to private school-much less me—if things kept breaking down around the "god damn" place. Mama remained calm and cool, then casually announced one night before dinner that she had found a part-time job—one she could work while Nancy was in school. Mrs. Dawkins, she went on, would take care of me.

"When did you arrange all of this?" Daddy asked her.

"Last week," she answered matter of factly.

"How are you going to get there?"

"The car."

"How will I get to work?"

Mama smiled at him. "The bus."

"We need to talk."

They must have never talked—either that or have not talked too long. Nancy said Mama would get her way so neither of us were all too surprised when Mama announced their plans for us not long afterwards. The first Tuesday after Labor Day, Nancy would take the bus to school. Mama and I would walk her to the corner to catch it and would be there when she was dropped off. Mrs. Dawkins had agreed to watch me during the mornings while Mama was at work. "How long will you have to work?" Nancy whined one afternoon.

"Just for a little while," she answered. "Will you be all right?"

Mama laughed. "Of course I will. Don't be silly."

"Why do you have to work anyway? You didn't have to before."

"Let's just say Daddy needs me to. Now don't either of you two worry. Nothing's going to change. I'll go and come home before you even miss me. You'll see."

"What about the man?" Nancy asked.

"Sheriff Wade will be watching and so will his men. They're not going to let you out of their sight. They promised. And when you get off that bus, I'll be there. So see. There's nothing for you to worry about. Okay?"

Even though the Tuesday after Labor Day seemed far off, the thought of it hanging in the near distance drove Jim Bill, Nancy and I into our own familiar world even more. It was one we knew that was destined never to last. Nancy's and Jim Bill's school, my going to Mrs. Dawkins and Mama's new job were all new and hostile factors which together would soon spell our world's doom. This vague, unspoken realization made our last days before Labor Day bittersweet. It was our way of spending time with a dying, best friend.

These days began early and ended late. What few flowers we could find were put on Dottie's East Texas grave marker each day, and Nancy and Jim Bill took to their play lines again. This time, though, they included me in their homespun skits. As usual, they were always the two stars. My roles always took the form of some type of non-talking animal or a character whose presence was at best unimportant to their plot. After two days of this I finally gave up. Nancy and Jim Bill both did the same shortly thereafter.

The idea to explore our second backyard was Nancy's. It was the remedy for a listless afternoon, which had thus far been whiled away by checkers and Parcheesi. Our backyard was halved by a broken-down, wooden fence, the back section of which we had been forbidden to enter. Daddy would occasionally mow parts of it when the weeds got too high, but to us it was a different world that we had chosen, before today, never to enter.

"Maybe we'd better stay out," I said as all three of us walked up to the fence and peered between the boards. The weeds and Johnson grass were knee-high, and in the back right corner of the lot was a mound of rotting boards, jagged scrap-metal and pieces of broken glass. Next to the mound a peach tree was growing, its crimson fruit swaying in the mid-afternoon breeze.

"Let's go get us some peaches," Jim Bill said. "Looky, we can get through right here." Jim Bill took the lead and Nancy and I followed. "Careful where you walk," he said. "Ants everywhere."

We worked our way back to the peach tree. Unlike our cottonwood, it stood no more than fifteen feet high. Ripened peaches dangled from the ends of its drooping limbs, "I'll get us some," Jim Bill said. "Wait here." He scampered up two of the heavier branches and before long was throwing fruit down to us. "That enough?" he asked us.

"Two more," Nancy said. "Those look good," she said pointing.

She was leaning over to catch her last peach from Jim Bill when she tripped. She tried to catch herself but landed on her hands and knees at the rubble's fringe. She screamed and grabbed her knee. She rolled over quickly—the board was still attached.

"She's fallen on a board!" I yelled. "It's stuck to her!"

Jim Bill jumped down from the tree. Nancy was screaming "My knee! My knee!"

"Be still, Nancy. It'll be okay." Jim Bill and I looked. Three of the board's nails had stabbed her knee. Two of them were partially in her knee while the third and largest one had gone all the way through. Nancy tried to pull it out but it wouldn't come.

"I'm going to go get Daddy!" I yelled. No sooner had I turned toward the house when I saw Daddy running towards us. He leaped the fence yelling "What's the matter? What's wrong?"

"It's Nancy!" I yelled back. "She's fallen on a board. It's stuck to her!"

Daddy ran up to Jim Bill and Nancy.

"She's startin' to turn white, sir. It's stuck in her knee. One of them's pretty deep!"

Daddy took the board and pulled it hard. Nancy cried in out in pain. Daddy pulled again. This time the board finally came lose.

"One of you run to the house. Tell Mama to call the doctor. Get some blankets, too! Daddy looked into her eyes. They rolled back into her head then shut. "She's passed out!" Daddy yelled. 'We've got to get her inside!

He lifted her up and began carrying her. When we got to the fence Daddy screamed in pain. "Brush them off, son! Hurry! I can't put your sister down!"

I looked at Daddy not realizing what he meant.

"The ants, son! Brush them off my legs!"

His brown trousers were covered with what looked like hundreds of ants. They had gotten inside and were stinging him terribly. Mama suddenly appeared and ran up to us. "Take her!" Daddy said as he lifted Nancy over the fence to Mama.

"She's cold!" Mama cried out.

"Try to keep her head down! We don't want her going into shock!"

Jim Bill ran to us carrying some blankets, and Mama wrapped Nancy in them as tightly as she could. "Bring her inside!" Sweat poured from Daddy's face as he stripped off his trousers. His legs were a mass of red welts. He slapped the ants off of him as best he could then ran inside.

Within half an hour Nancy's knee had swelled to the size of Jim Bill's football. Dr. Berger was on his way but Mama was frantic and kept yelling for Daddy. She finally told Jim Bill to go get his mother. She wrapped Nancy in blankets and propped her in a sitting position on one of the living room chairs. Mama bent Nancy's head below her waist and ordered me to keep her that way. Nancy was still cold and lifeless but I held her as close to me as I could to keep her warm. Her head bobbed to the left then to the right. She'd try to straighten up but I wouldn't let her. She would let out a moan, then sink again and bob back and forth some more.

Mrs. Dawkins came running and immediately took my place holding Nancy. "Find your father!" she yelled at me. "And hurry!" I ran through the house and finally found Daddy. He lay sprawled on the hallway floor as though he had been hit over the head with a hammer. I screamed for Mama. "Oh my God!" Mama yelled as she saw him. "Look at his legs!"

When Dr. Berger arrived Mama didn't know where to send him first. Nancy had begun vomiting but Daddy was still passed out. Dr. Berger ran back and forth shouting instructions to Mama and Mrs. Dawkins on how to treat the patient he wasn't with at the time. He kept asking how they looked and had their breathing or color changed. He gave Daddy a shot and Nancy one, too. He finally told Mama to call an ambulance.

A few minutes later we heard the dull screeching of its siren in the distance. Daddy was starting to come to but still didn't know where he was. Mama grabbed a folding chair from the kitchen, and Dr. Berger helped Daddy to his feet. He told him to sit down on it and stay put. "Make sure he doesn't fall off, son," he said turning to me. "Hold him on it real tight now."

The ambulance arrived and the driver and his helper loaded both Nancy and Daddy into it. Mama said she would follow in the car and told me to gather up some clothes—in case I needed to spend the night with the Dawkins'. She would pick me up when she got home from the hospital.

A short time later, Mrs. Dawkins and Jim Bill went home and the chaos and frenzy of that afternoon at 1854 Garrett Street finally subsided into an empty, eerie silence. The only sound was the strangely welcomed drone of our battling water cooler in the kitchen, which the heat and even Mr. Dawkins had finally turned on again. I picked up an old pair of blue jeans from my bedroom floor and a white, cotton tea shirt from the dresser drawer. Something told me the day's events had brought the final act of this summer's play to an end for us. A reluctance to say good-bye brought a lump to my throat as I opened the front door then closed it behind me. I remember trying to fight the tears back as I walked under our cottonwood and across the street. I felt like I was crying inside but refused to let it show. After all, I was going to Jim Bill's.

CHAPTER 18

Both Nancy and Daddy arrived home early the next morning, Nancy in a white, plaster-of-Paris cast that stretched from her upper left thigh down to her foot. Daddy let out a few choice words as he struggled to lift her from the ambulance. He had gotten one of his coat pockets stuck on the car's inside door handle and, in the process of trying to get loose, had yanked the wrong way and ripped the pocket almost off.

Despite the fact that he seemed to be his old self, Daddy was the main reason for their one-night lay over at the hospital. He had been bitten over seventy-five times and had collapsed again shortly after their arrival. The hospital doctors said if Dr. Berger had not have given him a shot, Daddy's reaction to the bites probably would have killed him.

Mama always told Nancy and me that there was something good to be found in almost everything, even though it might appear to be bad at the time. In my eyes, the good that came from Nancy's accident surfaced shortly after Daddy laid her on our living room couch. "Go get her crutches from the driver," he told me. I did like he said and soon viewed the stubby, rubber-tipped sticks as though they were a new toy. "Get off of them!" Mama said. "They're not for you. Go lay them over there by your sister."

What appeared to be the most good of all was Mama and Daddy's announcement that Nancy would not be able to attend school for at least two weeks. She was to stay off her feet as much as possible to allow her knee to heal properly. I was told I would be her nursemaid while Mama was at work, which I knew would suit Nancy just fine. Mama promised she would rescue me from what I could see coming as soon as she got home from work. If either of us needed any help, Mama went on, Mrs. Dawkins would be just across the street. All I needed to do was call her and she'd be right over.

"What about the man?" Nancy would ask.

"Sheriff Wade or someone from his department will be keeping an eye on the house," Daddy assured her. "Don't worry. Everything will work out fine."

The final days of the year's long, hot August came and, like a ghost, disappeared. Daddy returned to work, and Jim Bill marched off to school, football in hand. Nancy was almost nice to me and, much to my surprise, only mildly demanding. Mama had brought home some schoolbooks for Nancy to get acquainted with so she wouldn't fall too far behind. Nancy spent a lot of her time delving into their deep, dark pages and many times would ask me to sit next to her so she could provide me with a line-by-line explanation of what she had thought she learned. When I became bored, she'd get even by telling me to surprise Mama when she got home by doing this or doing that. I succumbed to her schoolwork, at last realizing that all she wanted was her little brother next to her—someone who she thought cared.

Three days after Mama started her new job, the Dawkins' received a phone call, and within a matter of hours, the two of them appeared in their driveway, suitcases in hand.

"Where are they going?" Nancy asked looking out at them from our living room window.

"Mrs. Dawkins' father had a heart attack last night. He is very ill," Mama answered. "There going to Brady, Texas to be with him."

"Is he going to die?" I asked.

Mama shrugged her shoulders. "I hope not. You might say a little prayer for him though." Mama's prayer request to us was her standard answer when she came up against something over which she had no control. She was deeply religious but also practical with her faith. She often used it to squash questions, the answers to which she did not know or want to deal with at the time.

Mama and Daddy left for work again the following morning. It was pouring down rain, and Mama was going to drive Daddy to the bus stop and wait with him until his bus came. The previous night, Warren Culbertson had said to expect rain for several days. A hurricane had made landfall near New Orleans and was heading slowly inland. He said it would drift north and west towards our area and that it would be a while before we saw the sun again.

Mama and Daddy kissed us good-bye then opened the front door. The rain was pelting down, and water was blowing in everywhere. A strong gust of wind suddenly hit the front door, and it flew open and crashed against the wall behind it. "Damn it!" Daddy said finally grabbing the doorknob. "You kids be careful and lock up after we leave. You know our numbers if you need us." With that they left. We heard the car start, then die, and then start again. We saw it back out of the driveway onto Garrett Street. The car stopped for a moment. Its lights came on, and then it slowly inched forward. We watched it as it finally disappeared from view, leaving behind our dimly lit house amongst the howling wind and the drenching rains. It also left behind the last few remnants of peace and tranquility which Nancy and I would experience for some time to come.

By 9:00 am the same morning, Nancy abandoned her books for Captain Kangaroo. She said her eyes were already tired and that she needed to rest. She told me to get the Parcheesi set—that beating me again might do her good. I was walking to the hall closet to get the gameboard when the telephone rang.

"Get it!" Nancy yelled. "It might be Mama."

My hello was met with an eerie silence on the other end. I heard somebody breathe twice into the mouthpiece, then there was a click followed immediately by the dial tone.

"Who was it?" Nancy asked as I set the game board in front of her.

"No one."

"Someone on the party line or maybe the storm," she concluded. "There it goes again. Run and answer it."

"Hello?"

No answer.

"Hello?"

No answer—just the breathing again. "Hello?" Silence, the click, the dial tone.

"Same thing as the last time," I told Nancy. "No one was there." An 'I'm afraid' sign flashed across her face then disappeared.

Our first game of Parcheesi ended as predicted. Nancy's reds and yellows were HOME long before my blues and greens were even close to their final destination.

"Maybe we should call Mama," she said midway through our second game.

"About what?"

"Those phone calls—they scare me—what if it's him?"

"Maybe we'd better. I'll call her right now." I ran to the phone and picked up the receiver. "It won't work," I yelled to her. "I can't get any dial tone!" I tried again and again but the line was dead. I ran back to the living room to Nancy. She sat motionless, not saying a word. "What's wrong with you? Didn't you hear me?"

She immediately put her hand to my mouth to shut me up. She pointed to the living room window. The figure of a man peered in for a split second then left. He was heading for the front door.

"It's him!" she said. "It's the man!"

Nancy looked at the door and immediately let out a gasp. She tried to run to it but fell. "The lock!" she cried out. "It's not locked!"

I ran to it and, reaching, turned the lock—not a second too soon. The bell rang once, then rang again. The doorknob turned. I ran back to Nancy and we huddled on the living room floor, waiting.

"What are we going to do?" she whispered as tears came to her eyes. Her fingers were tearing into my sides.

"We've got to see who it is!" I whispered to her. "Wait here. Be quiet!"

I crawled on my stomach towards the window and waited. Suddenly there was silence—then a large bang against the door. The wood frame tore lose, and the door slammed open. Nancy screamed. I flew towards the figure with my eyes closed. He caught me in mid-air then separated me from him with his arms.

"Hold on, son!" he said. "It's just me—Sheriff Wade!"

Daddy was outraged at Wade, and Mama, usually passive, tongue-lashed him ruthlessly. Despite the sheriff's logical explanations—no parent home, no phone calls answered, then dead phone lines—scaring Daddy's kids to death was the last straw.

"What else was I supposed to do?" he asked Daddy shortly afterwards. "I thought they were in trouble! Those cut phone lines told me something—despite the storms. I feared for their safety, sir, and acted accordingly."

The carpenter Wade sent out the next day to mend our front door wasn't the likes of Officer Bradley. He was quiet, and his hands shook all the time. Daddy stayed home from the office to supervise this man's work the best he could. The carpenter finally left shortly after noon without saying a word. Daddy saw him leave then got his own tools. He would spend the rest of the day trying to be sure the dead bolt fitted the undersized hole this carpenter had drilled.

CHAPTER 19

Three days had come and gone but still Jim Bill and his Mama had not shown up. Nancy and I would sit by ourselves on the couch and peer across the street, waiting for them to arrive. Their house lay like a vertical tombstone against the burnt-down houses water-leveled by the recent storms. These were the times we especially missed Dottie. She would have nestled up to us and known how we felt.

Nancy's leg was healing but the process was slow. Her fall made it bleed again. Daddy took her to Dr. Berger's office where the doctor checked both Daddy and Nancy. Dr. Berger became angry and told Daddy in no uncertain terms that Wade ought to be hung. Dr. Berger backed off the next day when Wade paid him a visit.

The telephone wires were reconnected shortly after our last Sheriff Wade incident, and our party line was restored to normal working order. Nancy seemed on the surface to be at ease and calm, but I could tell it was all a big show. Even when Mama and Daddy were home, she would jerk nervously when the telephone rang. "The man" was in the back of her mind much as the cut telephone wires were in the back of Daddy's. He had told Mama to quit work, but Mama reluctantly refused. She was the one who had to pay the bills.

Mama called us every other hour from her work place to see how we were doing. My responses were always the same: "Just fine, Mama. We're fine. No, no one's called. No, the Dawkins' aren't home yet. We're watching TV. We're playing Parcheesi" or "We're playing Checkers. Yes, Nancy's leg has quit its throbbing." I knew Mama was as tired of asking these same questions over and over again as I was of answering them, but I realized it was the only way she knew to ease the anxiety she felt by being separated from us.

The sun finally came out full force the first Friday after Labor Day. Mama threw open the windows for a few minutes before she left for work. The air was clear and calm, and its sweet fragrance set all of us in a better mood. Nancy's knee felt good enough for her to try her crutches. Before they left for work, both Mama and Daddy followed her around the house as she inched her way from room to room. They finally departed once they felt she had somewhat mastered walking on her extended, wooden pegs. Nancy spent a lot of that morning practicing on her crutches. She'd bob up and down on them, first in the hallway, then in the bedrooms and finally out in the living room again. She was just passing through the hallway for the hundredth time when the telephone rang. She picked up the receiver. "Hi, Mama," she said without thinking. "I've really learned how to use my crutches. Mama? Mama, is that you? Hello? Hello!"

"They hung up," she said dropping the receiver from her hands. "Oh God," she yelled. "It's him again!"

I ran to her and hung up the receiver. The phone rang again. I answered it. "Hi, Mama. We're fine. Did you just call and hang up?"

Mama's voice quivered then leveled out to a matter-of-fact tone. "No, Dear, but everything is fine. Be sure the doors are locked. I'm going to call Sheriff Wade. Wait for him. Daddy and I will be there shortly too."

"Are the doors locked?" Nancy whimpered.

"I'm sure they are—but I'll check one more time. Be quiet and wait here. I'll right back." I held my breath as I slid my way first to the front door then to the back door. All the locks were in place. I crawled over to the TV and turned it off, then went back to Nancy.

We listened. The silence gave way only to the merciless drone of the water cooler. We waited and watched and listened.

"Hail Mary, full of grace," Nancy started.

"Hush!" I told her. "Something's wrong!"

"Oh, God," she whispered in terror. "The water cooler's stopped! He's turned it off!"

I ran to the phone and tried to call Mama. There wasn't any dial tone—the line was dead.

"Come on!" I yelled at her. "We'll lock ourselves in the bathroom!" I tried to help Nancy to her feet but she was heavy. She fell against the half-open bathroom door and split her eyebrow wide open. It began bleeding as we closed the bathroom door behind us and locked it.

"Here. Hold this on your eye," I whispered shoving a washcloth into her hand.

"And be quiet!"

We heard a rough pulling and shoving at the front door handle then it quit.

"Where is he?" Nancy asked pushing her back harder against the bathroom wall.

"Shhh—listen! There's the screen door—He's gone to the back!"

We heard several, short, powerful blows against the backdoor and heard its wood frame splintering. Finally, the whole door crashed open. Then there was silence again.

"He's inside," I said. "I can hear him walking around."

The footsteps were heavy and unrythmic, as though he were dragging a leg. They went past the bathroom door into Nancy's room, then past it again into my room. We heard them approaching our bathroom door where they stopped. We saw the doorknob turn twice in either direction then heard his body slam against the door. It bulged on its hinges but held.

"The window!" Nancy said. "Try the window!"

"It's nailed shut!" I said trying to force it open. "Daddy nailed it shut!"

Nancy yelled out in desperation and called for Dottie as the door finally gave way. He looked at us then threw me aside. It was Nancy he was after. I grabbed his leg and bit it hard. He hit me on the head then hit me again. I held on and bit harder. My teeth sunk into his leg's flesh and his blood in my mouth repulsed me. I heard it rage loudly, like a wild animal that had been wounded. I felt it grab the back of my neck as it tried hard to pull me off. I grabbed his leg even harder, and he screamed out in pain as I sunk my teeth into him deeper. He kicked lose, picked me up and threw me through the air. I hit the tile above our bathtub and lay there half-dazed. The room was spinning as I looked around. I remember seeing him pick Nancy up from the floor. She was limp and lifeless. Oh, God, I remember thinking—she's dead.

A strange, gray fog started whirling around me. Dottie died again. The cottonwood collapsed with the wind, and swirling memories of planes at Love Field entered my mind. Mama said good-bye—Daddy said hello—and Jim Bill warned us—the ants. Dottie barked, the owl sang, and Jonathan spoke through the clouds. LD appeared and was suddenly gone then Officer Bradley came with the headstone, then the Stewart's with Jaspar and Ortiz. Then came the fire, then the ambulance then, all of sudden, nothing came at all.

CHAPTER 20

There was rumored to be a legend regarding the Wild Man of the Trinity River. He was purported to be half-man, half animal, shaggy in appearance, hunchbacked and rather huge in size. He roamed up and down the secluded, over-grown banks of the Trinity occasionally flashing in and out of sight. Jim Bill told us about him and swears he'd seen him once or twice. In our imaginations, our captor could have easily been mistaken for this man-thing. Being stunned and shocked at his attack, our minds caught different first images of him which we'd hash and rehash for many years to come. Big and hairy, hunched-back and foaming at the mouth, it really was irrelevant at that time. He had sprung his trap and caught us. For some reason, I was the tag-along. Nancy was his prey.

He had stowed us on the concrete floor of a large, empty room. Only a small, outside window draped by cobwebs looking like dusty lace lighted the chamber. The opening lay a little below the ceiling line, and, because of its dinginess, it emitted hardly any outside moonlight at all.

When I came to I found myself sprawled belly-down on the hard, cool floor. My head ached, and there was a terrible taste in my mouth. I spit several times trying to get rid of it. There were pieces of sinews between my teeth, and I gagged when I finally realized these were small bits of the muscle and tissue I had bitten off the man-thing's leg during the attack.

I rose to a sitting position and peered into the murky darkness. I felt around on the floor, hoping Nancy was somewhere close when I heard a low moan. "Nancy," I whispered. "Are you there?"

She moaned again. My fingers fumbled toward the direction I thought her groans came from, and I finally found her leg. I crawled up beside her and touched her face. "Are you okay?"

"My leg," she answered. "It really hurts."

"Just lie there and be still."

"Where are we?"

"Some sort of basement somewhere. He must have thrown us in here then left. Listen—can you hear it? It sounds like water."

The sound was muffled but recognizable. It was water lapping against the building.

"We must be by a pond or lake or something. Be quiet. Play dead. He's coming!"

His footsteps approached from somewhere outside the room. We heard the jingle of keys and the click of a lock. The door slowly creaked open. Framed against a dimly lit background was a massive human figure, his silhouette filling almost the entire opening. He suddenly flipped the door open the rest of the way. It banged loudly against the inside wall. He stood motionless and peered into the room, his breathing loud and strained. I heard my heart pounding in my head. It was so loud I was sure he could hear it too. It was all I could do to keep from crying out.

He grunted something under his voice, then he began limping slowly towards us. Nancy could see him, too. She let out a short, muffled cry, and he suddenly stopped. He tilted his head as though trying to figure out where Nancy's voice came from, then began walking slowly towards us again.

I was lying directly in his path between him and Nancy. I could tell he could see the darkness of her body against the floor, but his focus was so intent on her that he instinctively walked around me then tried to sit down next to her. He went to one knee, then to all fours, shifting his weight so that he could easily rock backward to a sitting position. His balance gave way, and he fell sideways on his other leg.

"M' god!" he thundered, grabbing his leg." He whimpered several times as he lay clinching his calf and writhing in agony. I felt something wet and warm oozing its way from my cheek towards my mouth and moved my head away from it. I glanced at him and saw that his pants leg was torn and drenched in a dark, wet liquid. He was still bleeding from my bite, and I was swimming in his blood. As suddenly as it had started, his seizure stopped. He lay there limp and lifeless.

My first instinct was to grab Nancy and run, but I waited. He wasn't out—just in pain. He began rolling, first to his left, then to his right, then finally sat up. Saliva dripped from his mouth until he finally sucked most of it inside. He wiped the rest of it away with his shirtsleeve.

He sat down next to Nancy then pulled from inside his wrinkled, stained shirt a battered, beat-up parcel.

"I want t' read 'em to you maself," he grunted. "Ma love letters. Yu've seem 'em afore but it's ok. Hear 'em from me tonite." Your daddy or dog ain't 'round so's I can tell ya' m'self. Ma' hand print ain't so good. You figur'd that b' now". He laughed out loud then forget himself and moved his leg.

"Ma god," he roared. "I's sounds like that old, weak mule when I got to him. Feel like 'im too," he snorted looking at his leg. "G'ess it must of hurt 'im real good."

He clutched his bleeding leg then roled his eyes. He sat there for what seemed an eternity—a stone statue. Then he looked down. "M' leg! It's bleedin' awful bad." He took in lots of air and then let it out like a tire with a slow leak. "Don't matter no how" he concluded. "Got these here luv letters that I'm goin' to read ta yu."

Nancy moaned again. He stroked her head. "J'st listen up here" he whispered in her ear. "This is the one your father punished that hell bitch dog for Christmas night. "Listen real good," he said gently shaking her head by the hair.

"'Nuz paper picture was so rare caught my love in your hair. I love you, so much—without compare.'" He stopped then took a huge breath. "What do ya think?" he whispered in her ear, stroking her hair.

She didn't answer.

He raised her by her hair, looked into her face, then let her head down again. "Just My furst my furst tr'. Here's ma next letr t' you. "'Tried to kill that black bitch—all 'cause of ma' luv fur you. That mangy ol' dog bit me and I felt hurt and then i's gone. But I luv ya jest the same—anyway." He waited for Nancy's response. Nothing. "They gets alots bet'r." he grunted.

He swooned back and forth until he finally lost his balance and fell to his side. He roared in pain, then, after a minute began to whimper. He finally struggled to a sitting position again. Saliva was now flowing freely from his mouth. He wiped it off on his shirtsleeve and finally started up again. "Here's another one—ma best un 'cept for un more." he grunted: "Fire fire, real bright ta see. Made 'em chicks run and fly. The fire—like ma luv fer you."

He paused and ran the worn papers between his fingers.

He let out some short, low half-laughs like he was remembering what happened with the coop.

"Ma last 'n," he uttered. "wrote 't 'ust for y' tonite—ma bestest too. Just ya wit and see: 'Queen Nancy 'f ma hart, ma luv is so deep, jest as th' lake ou'side.'" He looked at her. "Liken to all that? Hold on. Thar's more: 'Yur Daddy's l'l brown-hared gurl—East'r Queen-that's you. Now ya'll be ma queen fer taday, and for all the time ta come.'" His face grimaced as he peered down at Nancy waiting for her reaction. Still there was none.

He strained to his feet and started pacing back and forth. His limp got worse and worse until he finally dropped slowly to one knee in front of her. He tore into the papers and thrust them into her face. "Cum on!" he yelled down at her. "Dun all th's for 'ou and all ya can do is 'ust lie thur likin' ya was dead?"

Still she didn't react.

He grabbed her hair and yanked her head up so he could look at her. Her eyes were shut, and she seemed limp. He shoved her head away. It hit the floor with a thud.

"All thu trouble jest fer nothin! 'ou wait rite 'ere!" he uttered. "I'm goi' ta fix you good. 'est wait an' see."

He limped to the door, looked at the love notes he was holding, then stopped. He threw them to the ground, unzipped his fly and urinated on them. "I'm goi' ta fix you good!" he roared. "'est you wait an' see."

His silhouette disappeared as he slowly closed and locked the door behind him. I heard his footsteps become fainter and fainter until they finally faded into silence.

"Nancy! Nancy!" I half-way yelled, shaking her. "Come on—he's coming back—we've gotta get out of here!"

I heard her sigh, then saw her face. Her eyes were wide open but something was wrong.

"Nancy!" I said tapping her face. "Come on! Come on!" It was then I noticed. She was staring right at me but couldn't see.

She lay motionless for a long second then her eyes suddenly flashed hurriedly around the room. Finally, they came back to me again. She recognized me this time and began sobbing like I've never seen her do before.

"At least your with me now," I whispered to her, trying to calm her down. "You scared me there for a minute. I didn't know what you were up to." She laid her head in my lap and sobbed some more. Finally, she sat up and wiped her eyes. "You've got to leave me and go get some help," she whispered in half-after-crying breaths. "Run! Get out of here before he comes back!"

"I'm not leaving you here by yourself with him."

"It's our only chance."

"I'm not leaving you alone!" I said. "Don't say anything more about it! Besides, couldn't even if I wanted to. He's locked the door and taken the key."

"Oh, God!" she said grabbing my shirt. "He's going to kill us!"

The thought of being killed had never entered my mind until Nancy said it. It seemed like an impossibility that we would end up dead. Even my worst nightmares hadn't ended like that. "We're not going to die," I assured her. "We've just got to think of a way to get out of here, that's all. We've got to figure out a plan."

There was silence for a minute. "First I've got to see if I can walk," she said. "Try to help me up." I stood up and grabbed underneath her arms and lifted. She struggled to get her good leg underneath her. "Come on, a little more! Good. You're up. Quit leaning on me so much or we're both going to fall! See if you can walk a little on your hurt leg."

She gradually shifted her weight to it then took a small step forward. "It hurts," she said.

"But can you walk on it?"

"A little," she answered.

"Hang on to me—we're going over behind the door."

"Why?"

"Just let's go."

We limped our way across the room until we found the door.

"Lean here against the wall. When he opens the door, it's going to open to the inside. He probably won't be able to see too good at first because of the dark. I'm going to try and kick his hurt leg. Then we're going to run."

"That's the stupidest plan I've ever heard," Nancy said. "How are we going to get away? He's faster than we are! I can't run anyway!'

"Well, when I kick him he'll probably fall. His leg's bleeding, and he's hurting pretty bad. Maybe that'll slow him up enough for us to get out. You just make sure you get through the door as fast as you can."

Nancy's silence was broken only by the lazy lapping of the water against the room's outside wall. She had evidently okayed my plan for the lack of a better one. Frightened and alone, we held each other's hands for what seemed like an eternity. We whispered that Mama and Daddy would find us and wished Jim Bill was there to help us. Finally Nancy sank to a sitting position. She couldn't stand any longer. It seemed we were floating in the room's darkness, half-suspended between conscious terror and nagging fatigue. We waited endlessly for the thing to return, for his footsteps and his arrival. We would not be disappointed.

CHAPTER 21

It was a sliver of light on the concrete floor—hardly recognizable at first. I stared at it, barely paying any attention to it at all until my swooning senses returned. I felt Nancy's hand clutch my arm and squeeze. She knew what it was—the door had been unlocked and cracked open slightly. We had heard no footsteps, no click of the door lock. We waited in silence and held our breaths.

"Let's go," I finally whispered to Nancy. "Maybe he's gone." Nancy shook her head.

"Come on!" I urged her again. "Now's our chance!"

Nancy shook her head again; her eyes open wide with fright. "He's waiting for us out there," she whispered. "I know he is. I just know it."

A few moments later, the door swung open a little more then stopped again. We stayed our ground, fighting back our panic through the uncertainty and the silence. Suddenly, we heard him. He was right outside the door. His breaths were short and restrained as though he were trying to mask them.

"Come 'n," we heard him whisper. "Yu two come 'n out 'ere."

Nancy and I looked at each other wondering what to do. "Got sometin' fo yu", he said louder. "Sum food and sum wat'r. Sumthin' else speciel too. Cum on out—I ain't goin' to hurt yu. Really I ain't."

His voice sounded kind and soft. He opened the door a little more and threw two boxes of candy a short way into the inside doorway. "Gots lots mo' too," he added. "Cum on out here," he coaxed. "God knows I ain't got the stength ta hurt yu no mo. Ma leg! It's bleedin' awful like. You'se have ta hel' me. I mite just die own ya rite here. It hurts so bad!"

"He's dying for sure," I whispered to Nancy. "Now's our chance," I said starting to creep towards the door, but Nancy pulled me back again.

"He's not dying," Nancy scolded. "He's trying us. How stupid can you be!"

"What yu sayin'? I can her' yu talkin'. Yu got tu believ' me. I didn't want to hurt nobody—not yu or yur dog, or that black woman or ev'n the wetback or his animul. I did it all fur yu, gurl—becuze of ma luv fer yu. I ain't a mean man. Jus' a sufferin' one. Ma lessen's been lerned. Yu got to hel' me—ma leg. If'n they catch me, there goin' ta lock me up or maybe do things ev'n badder. I ain't ev'r had nothin' 'til I saw yu, lil gurl. Nev'r will, nev'r will 'gain. Cum own out her' an' hep a dyin' ol' man."

We waited.

"I got some things fer you too. Like I said 'fore. Looky her'. Sum mor'" A few more boxes of candy landed on the floor.

"I'll buy ya a new doggie if ya want. If ya cum I won't lay a hand on ya either. I'll r'turn yu to you' folks and show yu how to get ther'. Then I'll leave and yu'll nev'r be bothered b' me 'gain. Yu got ta hurry, though. I'm feelin' so bad and hurtful. I think I's goin' to die right her'. Yu dun't want to be th cause o' my dyin', does yu?. Cum on. Kids. I need yur help."

His voice tailed off. Silence once again overwhelmed the room. The breathing stopped; the door stood still; no more candy littered the grey floor. We waited and waited until we couldn't stand it any more. "Ma god!" his voice suddenly yelled out. "Ma god—help me rite now! I's dyin fur sure!"

"Let us see you die," Nancy suddenly called out. "Like our Dottie!"

"Bitch" was all we heard back.

"Bastard!" Nancy yelled back at him. "I hate you!" she answered. "You killed Mr. Ortiz and Jaspar and even our Dottie. I'll never ever like you."

"I knows. But I'm dyin' here soon. It don't matt'r no mo anyhow. I'm cumin thro this here door rite now with my surprise. Jest yu wait and see it."

He grunted and groaned. Within seconds we saw his massive shadow rise against the concrete floor. It took some steps forward and stopped after it had barely entered the room.

"Where is yu two," he thundered walking forward again. We held our breaths as we saw his figure advance in the dim light. His back was to us as he continued limping towards the middle of the room. In his right hand, he held a huge knife. Its long, silver blade flashed in the dim light as it swung back and forth with his rough gate. We stiffened against the wall, terrified. Nancy and I had discovered his surprise.

Our instincts screamed flight. Without saying a word, we grabbed each other's hands and headed through the doorway. Partway through it, Nancy lost her hold of me and fell. She screamed as he struggled slowly towards us trying to grab her leg. I kicked his hand away and looked for his bad leg. He had landed on his stomach, his head facing the door. His leg was not within kicking distance. He was trying to get up again as I struggled to drag Nancy through the doorway. She was using her good leg to help scoot herself through the entrance into the narrow hallway.

"Yu tu ain't goin' nowher'!" he yelled finally getting to his feet. "I got yu now! I got the both of yu now!" He lunged forward. My foot flew towards him and luckily hit full force on his wound. He screamed in pain and went down.

"Close the door,!" Nancy yelled. "Lock him in!"

I found the door's latch and tried to pull the door to, but he grabbed the edge of it with his hand and kept it from swinging closed. The door jolted the knife lose. The blade flew across the room. His hand slipped off the door's edge as he lunged after the knife. I pulled as hard as I could slamming the door shut.

"Lock it! Lock it!" Nancy cried.

I tried but the door flew open. Before us loomed the man-thing. He picked me up by my throat and pinned me against the wall.

"Stop it!" Nancy yelled. "I'll go with you! Just let him go!"

I dropped to the floor like a limp dishtowel. He swooned over Nancy and cradled her next to him. She yelled as he picked her up and carried her away. I saw their silhouettes disappear down the narrow hall. She was crying and fighting, and he was restraining her as best he could. "I hate you! I hate you!" she yelled as she fought him off. A door slammed open and then shut. I ran to the door and threw it open. I heard Nancy yell again. I called after her as loud as I could. I yelled again and again but there was no answer.

A warm breeze whisked by me—like a Jonathan breeze. I looked up and saw the clouds wisping past the full moon. LD flashed in and out of my mind. It was then I realized I was freed and outside.

I suddenly heard Nancy call again and followed her sounds. The undergrowth was thick and her calls close. I ran after her, tripping through the underbrush. Finally, I saw her. She was lying face down in the full moonlight, silent and still.

I looked around for him. He lurked in every night-shadow, behind every bush. Each rustling was his footstep, every night wind his breath. I talked to Nancy to bring her back, then finally gave up. I found a branch and swung it hard in the air. At least if he came back I could hit him with it, I thought. I sat up as long as I could and thought of Mr. Dawkins standing guard all night in our living room. Surely he must have felt like I did now—praying for a menace not to show up, wondering what to do if he did.

CHAPTER 22

I dreamed God had come and saved us. It was a good dream but a strange one. He was carrying me in his arms; yet when I looked up I couldn't see his face. I felt no sense of relief or release of anxiety, just a deep realization that despite the person in whose arms I was, Nancy and I were still in deep trouble. It was a nightmare more than anything else, and it's reality startled me. I felt my body jump, and I soon found myself sitting where I had fallen asleep. Nancy still lay motionless beside me. The wind swayed the trees' limbs back and forth. I remembered the man-thing and began to cry. The nightmare I had awoken to was worse than the one I had just dreamed.

The moon had not yet set. Its beams reflected off of the large body of water in front of me. I took off my shirt and went to the water's edge. I dipped it in the water than ran it over my face and head. I dipped it again then went back to Nancy. I rolled her over on her back and began patting her face with my shirt. Her eyes were closed shut, and I could see that her leg was bleeding again.

"Nancy," I whispered. "Wake up."

I went back the water and dipped my shirt in it again. I came back to her and Slowly dripped it over he face. The drops tracked down her forehead and cheeks to the ground below. She moved a bit, then moved again, and then jerked suddenly like she was startled. Her eyes opened gradually. She was groggy and disoriented. She looked at me then sat up slowly.

"What happened?" she mumbled. "Where are we?"

"We're outside the building someplace. He must have dropped you and went on. I found you lying here, knocked out."

Nancy looked around trying to remember when suddenly fear gripped her face. "Where is he? What happened to him?"

"Don't know," I answered. "He hasn't come back."

"Oh God!" she said. "What if he does? What will we do?"

"Found me a stick to hit him with." I answered. She looked past me like she always did when one of my answers was stupid.

"How long do you think we've been here?" she asked.

"I don't know. Maybe two or three hours or so. I don't think daylight's going to come anytime soon. Least not for a couple of more hours."

"Then we'd better leave here and go hide somewhere else.

If he comes after us again he'll come right back here where he dropped me. Help me get up."

Nancy and I tried to get her to her feet as best we could, but it took several times. Her body was stiff, and her sore leg could hardly stand any weight on it. When we finally stood upright we headed away from the building and the water towards the woods. The underbrush tugged at our legs like it was dead-set on making us fall down. The vines and branches from the trees scratched our arms and faces as we inched forward. Suddenly, after a few more paces, the trees and underbrush parted and before us stretched a narrow, two-lane road. Nancy started hurting something awful as the cast on her hurt leg turned darker and darker with new blood. We finished crossing the road and found a small clearing where we finally decided to rest. From it we could see the road, the building and the spot we had just left. I took my wet shirt and wrapped it around Nancy's cast. She looked at me. "That's really going to do a lot of good!" she said sarcastically.

"Don't want to look at it anymore," I whispered back. "It's making me feel sick."

The night hung on and on. We felt a little safer now that we had moved, but neither of us had any idea where we were or how we would ever escape. To make matters worse, the moon was starting to fade behind some approaching storm clouds. Soon it would be pitch black and pouring rain.

We could do nothing from our little hiding spot but watch and wait. Lightning flashed on the horizon followed by low distant rumbles of thunder. "Look!" Nancy suddenly whispered, pulling on my arm. "Look! Over there!"

Nancy had been right. The man thing had come back to where he had dropped her. He was limping listlessly through the trees and underbrush, half-grunting as he circled and circled trying to find us. He would stop when he encountered something on the ground thinking it was one of us, then mumble his disappointment as he slowly resumed his search. We could tell his leg was still nagging at him. He was favoring it almost to the point of falling with each step he took.

He suddenly stopped his wanderings and looked around as though he had picked up some scent in the air or heard something he was expecting to hear. His glance slowly turned to our left then to our right. Finally, it stopped directly on us.

"He sees us!" Nancy whispered.

"He can't see us," I argued back. "Not here! Be quiet!"

After a long second he resumed his search. The moon faded, and the storm rolled in. The wind howled through the trees as the driving rain continually stung us. Except for the lightning bolts the night was now pitch black. We continued to watch the spot hoping the storm would finally drive him away. The next bolt of lightning gave us heart. The storm we had dreaded had proven to be our friend. He had disappeared. The man-thing had abandoned his search.

We cramped together in our new hiding spot, shivering and shaking as the storm broke around us. We'd seen storms like this from our bedrooms before but being caught in one was a whole different experience. We had no pillows to throw over our ears or any blankets in which to curl up. We had no Dottie to call. We had all we could do to say where we were. Nancy said we should go into the building for shelter, then changed her mind. That was where he would be, she told me, just waiting for us to come in from the wind and rain.

We prayed together, and it seemed to do some good. The thunder abated as the wind became the storm's afterthought. The rains moved on also, changing themselves into a murky, drizzly mist. We looked at the spot again. Still he was not there. We saw more lightning in the distance and dreaded the thought of still another storm heading our way. We knew we would not be able to withstand it.

"We ought to move into the building," I told Nancy.

She shook her head. "I know he's there," she whispered. "I'd rather die out here."

I didn't answer but crouched down beside her, submitting to her last wish. The silence hung on the night like the mist in the air. It penetrated everything without saying a word. We sat and shook and chattered our teeth and watched and waited. A lightning bolt lit up the sky, and we saw him. He was leaning against the building gripping his leg.

"There!" Nancy yelled forgetting herself. "I see him!"

"Shut up! He'll hear us for sure!"

Nancy threw her hand to her mouth. She realized her mistake. "Oh, God," she uttered. "I've done it now."

She was right. His head jerked up like an animal who had just discovered its prey. He picked up his long knife from beside him and headed in our direction.

"I heard yu!" he yelled. "I knows wher' yu tu are. Don't yu worry, yu tu. I'm cumin! In a minut' I'll be thur in a hurry to rescu yu!" He said something else, I thought about Nancy, then his silhouette faded into the blackness. The second storm hit full force a few moments later. It was then, in our most desperate seconds, we noticed a strange light in the distance.

"Our guardian angel is coming to help us!" Nancy cried. sitting up. "Look! Look!" she yelled pointing. "Her light is getting brighter. I knew she'd come! I just knew she would!"

The rain was falling in torrents as I strained my eyes to see. The lights were getting brighter. I got up from our hiding place and walked towards the road. Something moved from across the way. It was the man thing. He was struggling to reach me before the angel did. I yelled and ran away from him towards the light. The light and the man thing were on a collision course, and I was in the middle. I held my breath and prayed to God for help. Nancy screamed. I closed my eyes and sank to my knees and let out one final yell.

She approached me in the mist as I sat half stunned in the middle of the road. At first I was sure Nancy was right. She was an angel or so it appeared—either that or the Lady the Savoys had told us about. The car lights behind her gave her a ghostly appearance as she neared, the wind transforming her dress into some type of heavenly gown like the ones I had seen on some holy cards.

"The man-thing," I uttered to her. "He's near!"

She didn't understand what I was saying. The storm was too loud. I turned to look behind me. That's when I saw him. The man-thing was lying face down by the side of the road no more than three feet away. His knife had dropped from his hand. He lay dead still.

She picked me up and carried me through the driving rain to the back seat of her car. "Nancy," I said to her. "Get Nancy. She's over there," I said pointing in the direction of the clearing. The lady left again. Within seconds Nancy and the lady appeared in the car's headlights. She placed Nancy next to me without saying a word. As we inched forward through the storm we passed the man-thing's body. His head moved, and he suddenly looked up. He raised to his knees and flailed his arms in the air. We were rescued, and he had lost. Sheriff Wade would later surmise he had been caught in his own trap, the victim of his basic need to possess and covet.

CHAPTER 23

A week later things were somewhat back to normal at 1854 Garrett Street. Nancy had surgery on her leg the night we were found. Despite this, Dr. Berger promised Mama and Daddy we would be just like new with a little rest.

The lady who rescued us never gave Mama and Daddy her name. Daddy said she was young and attractive, and, of course, because of the storm, dripping wet. In all of the commotion of our arrival, they didn't see her slip away. Daddy said she was there one minute and gone the next. "It was the Lady," Nancy said one night as we sat around our booth eating dinner. "Just like the Savoys had said."

"Oh, honey," Mama told her. "That was just a fairy tale."

Daddy looked at Mama then back down at his plate. "He did take them to the old fishery at White Rock," Daddy commented. "Almost makes you believe in fairy tales, doesn't it?"

The doorbell rang, and I ran to answer it. It was Sheriff Wade doing another one of his drop-bys. Daddy got up and shook his hand then asked him to pull up a chair. Mama's greeting was a little less friendly.

"Sorry to interrupt your dinner, but was in the neighborhood and thought I'd come on by. Glad this ordeal is over with. My, oh my. It was an ordeal, huh?"

His question was answered with silence. "Well, anyway I won't be too long," he said shifting in his chair. "Thanks to you kids, Mr. Boggs is now a free man. We let him lose yesterday. Never seen nobody so relieved and thankful. The real culprit is resting in the hospital. You took quite a chunk out of him, son."

"Sheriff Wade!" Mama objected. "We're eating."

"Beg you pardon, Ma'am, for that untimely remark. His name's Leon Simmons. Don't rightly know where he came from or where he's been 'til now. Anywise, the county psychiatrist ran some tests on him. Once he gets physically well the Judge wants him shipped to the mental hospital at Terrell. No need to elaborate. Let's just say he'll be in there for a mighty long time."

"Under guard," I hope Mama said.

"No need to worry, Ma'am. The road to Terrell is most always one way. Well," he said getting up, "I got another person to see 'fore I call it a day. I'll see myself out."

He went to the front door, opened it and then stopped.

"Apologize for makin' you all go through all this. Sometimes no matter how careful you plan, things don't always turn out."

"You did the best you could," Daddy answered. "We're just glad it's over."

"Ma'am," he said tipping his hat to Mama. "Miss," he said tipping his hat to Nancy. "Y'all have a good night."

Sheriff Wade steeped through the door and shut it behind him. We would read about him in the paper and occasionally see him on the news, but this had been his last visit to our home. It was his curtain call for our play, and even Mama admitted with some reservations that his exit had been staged with a touch of class certainly uncommon to the man we had come to know as Sheriff Wade.

The events surrounding Leon Simmons over the past few months had changed our lives. Nonetheless, life at 1854 Garrett Street still moved on. Jim Bill finally let me play football with him and Gary

Shouts, and he continued instructing Nancy and me daily on the ways of the southwest.

On weekends, we'd lay on our backs in our front yard watching the clouds pass overhead. Occasionally we'd see a Jonathan cloud and feel his breeze next to us, as LD had said, and we'd put flowers on Dottie's grave regularly. Jim Bill would always take it upon himself to test her marker. He said he felt it was his duty as her dying friend.

The summer, like the Lady, had quickly come and disappeared. It left behind our Dottie, LD, and Jim Bill's father, our neighbors' burnt-down houses, a charred coop, and Leon Simmons. Little did we realize then that the small, everyday pieces of this childhood experience would stay with us through the remainder of our lives.

We moved from 1854 Garrett Street three years later. Mama and Nancy cried, and even Daddy was upset. Nancy, Jim Bill and I put our last flowers on Dottie's grave, then went to the front yard where our folks were waiting. Nancy hugged Mrs. Dawkins, then turned to Jim Bill.

"Jim Bill," she said in front of us and looking right in his eyes. "I love you".

Jim Bill blushed and looked at his Mama. She smiled. "Can't blame her a bit," she answered. "Finally love requited!"

Jim Bill came over to me. He was much taller now. "Glad you finally learned how to read."

"Yea," I said, my voice breaking up. I didn't want to cry in front of Jim Bill. "It's so sad," I said. "We'll never see you again."

"Nonsense!" Daddy said. "We're not moving to another county, you know."

"Here's something for you. An arrowhead. Put it in your pocket. It's good luck."

"Thanks, Jim Bill," I answered. "I'll keep it with me all the time, but it won't be like having you with me though."

Jim Bill approached me. Tears were in his eyes.

"Why Jim Bill. You're crying," I said.

"Don't you ever know when to shut up!" Nancy whispered.

"I ain't one for dramatics, but your sister taught me some lines in your back yard that hit me right now. 'Partin' is both sweet and sour.' I mean the Good Lord didn't bless Mama and me with a little brother. Not until you." He reached down and hugged me to him. Mama and Daddy turned away.

"It's time to go," Daddy finally said. "Let's get in the car."

There were no storms on the horizon, and Leon Simmons had been put to rest. Daddy backed our car out of driveway, put it in gear and we started to pull away. Jim Bill stood in the middle of the street watching us go. Suddenly he waived his hands over his head. He wanted us to stop. Nancy yelled at Daddy, and our car came to a halt.

"I wanted to tell you," Jim Bill said running up to my window. "I made up that story about your dog. She never felt you didn't love her when she was dying. When you came out that night she waged her tail when she saw you. If the truth be known, she loved you more than me. That's all I wanted to say."

"What's he talking about?" Nancy asked.

"Don't know," I answered. Then I smiled.

Epilogue

Our old neighborhood on Garrett Street has long since succumbed to a dynamic city metropolis. Daddy's Interurban bus is by now a worn out piece of scrap metal, a fate with which he is undoubtedly pleased. Fitzhugh has widened; the side streets made straight. White Rock Lake is currently a recreational park, no longer the solitary reservoir for which it was originally known. Our family's short history on Garrett Street, like the unknown Lady, has vanished but reappears from time to time. Today it takes the forms of kids' lightning bugs in see through plastic jars, footprints in occasional snows, or even a genuine antlion burrowing its way through the black, Texas sod. Mr. Ortiz had also been right. The rag business in Dallas died with his and Jaspar's demise. Our old house has long since been demolished, but, remarkably, Dottie's marker is still there, as Wade promised it would be. Our grandfather cottonwood, too, has weathered the storm of progress. The wise old tree still caresses the north and south winds, his incessant and seasonal lovers. Yet, his silent wisdom goes all but unnoticed now.

Occasionally my business in the city will take me by 1854 Garrett Street. Most always, I'll climb from my car and greet my grandfather friend, and I'll silently reminisce about the times we have shared. I'll look up and see the white clouds floating their way south and see his green leaves dancing in the breeze. It's then that I'm suddenly home again and think of our days on Garrett Street.

About the Author

Alfred R. Pierotti, Jr. moved to Dallas with his parents and sister in 1947 and spent the next eight years growing up on Garrett Street. He earned his Bachelor of Arts and Masters Degrees at the University of Dallas in Irving, Texas. He spent the next three decades in the insurance business and began his teaching career in 1980 as a member of Eastfield College's adjunct faculty. He currently teaches Senior English at Jesuit College Preparatory School in Dallas.

0-595-22486-5

Printed in the United States
1052300004B